"You Americans are all alike," the sailor snarled

A moment later the Frenchman jerked a knife from the sheath at the small of his back and lunged.

Bolan blocked the thrust and knocked the blade aside. He caught his adversary's wrist and pulled the man toward him as his other fist crashed into the guy's face. Blood shot from his nostrils, splattering both men.

The Executioner held on as the sailor's head flew back, snapping like a whip. When an opening came, Bolan threw a short uppercut into the knifer's sternum. Air rushed from the guy's lungs. He slumped to the floor in a sitting position, then fell forward, cracking his head on the cold concrete.

As four other Frenchmen stood to enter the fray, Bolan drew the Desert Eagle and began to back toward the door.

From the corner of his eye he watched Gus Webster and Hugo Ulrikson. The two men sat calmly at the dark table in the corner, watching the show.

Both looked interested.

MACK BOLAN®

The Executioner

DON PENDLETON'S
THE EXECUTIONER®
FEATURING MACK BOLAN®

DEATH TRAIL

A GOLD EAGLE BOOK FROM
WORLDWIDE®

TORONTO • NEW YORK • LONDON
AMSTERDAM • PARIS • SYDNEY • HAMBURG
STOCKHOLM • ATHENS • TOKYO • MILAN
MADRID • WARSAW • BUDAPEST • AUCKLAND

First edition August 1992

ISBN 0-373-61164-1

Special thanks and acknowledgment to
Jerry VanCook for his contribution to this work.

DEATH TRAIL

there is always
a comforting thought
in the time of trouble when
it is not our trouble
—Donald R. P. Marquis
1878–1937

I've never gone looking for trouble. I never had to. It was always out there, waiting—looking for me, or anyone else who cared enough to confront it.
—Mack Bolan

THE
MACK BOLAN®
LEGEND

Nothing less than a war could have fashioned the destiny of the man called Mack Bolan. Bolan earned the Executioner title in the jungle hell of Vietnam.

But this soldier also wore another name—Sergeant Mercy. He was so tagged because of the compassion he showed to wounded comrades-in-arms and Vietnamese civilians.

Mack Bolan's second tour of duty ended prematurely when he was given emergency leave to return home and bury his family, victims of the Mob. Then he declared a one-man war against the Mafia.

He confronted the Families head-on from coast to coast, and soon a hope of victory began to appear. But Bolan had broken society's every rule. That same society started gunning for this elusive warrior—to no avail.

So Bolan was offered amnesty to work within the system against terrorism. This time, as an employee of Uncle Sam, Bolan became Colonel John Phoenix. With a command center at Stony Man Farm in Virginia, he and his new allies—Able Team and Phoenix Force—waged relentless war on a new adversary: the KGB.

But when his one true love, April Rose, died at the hands of the Soviet terror machine, Bolan severed all ties with Establishment authority.

Now, after a lengthy lone-wolf struggle and much soul-searching, the Executioner has agreed to enter an "arm's-length" alliance with his government once more, reserving the right to pursue personal missions in his Everlasting War.

1

Trouble hovered in the air like a bad smell.

Mack Bolan slid onto a bar stool, glancing past the bartender into a mirror to watch the action behind him.

Three men sat near the door to the street, wearing khakis, deep tans and crew-cut hair. Telltale bulges protruded from under their arms.

Two dozen men were scattered around the room, each looking as hard as the ones near the door.

Bolan continued to watch. The clientele didn't surprise him. The Golden Scorpion, on the wharf of Ostend, Belgium, wasn't a place where you took the wife and kids after church. It was a known hangout for thieves, prostitutes and out-of-work mercenaries.

The bartender pulled his arms from the soapy water in the sink and looked up at Bolan.

"Beer," the Executioner said. "Stella."

The man nodded, dried his hands on a soiled dishrag and set a long-necked bottle on the bar.

Harsh laughter, broken by an occasional threat, rose above the hard-rock music that blasted from speakers positioned around the room. As he sipped at his beer, Bolan's practiced eyes flickered unnoticed to a large table near the hall to the rest room. A half-dozen drunks clad in the ringed T-shirts of the French navy were downing wine and beer.

A short, balding sailor with a wispy mustache suddenly stood up. With a loud cry, he threw his beer bottle against the brick wall. The glass shattered, raining down to the floor as the rest of the men roared with laughter.

Young waitresses maneuvered around the tables, their faces almost as weathered as the men. Premature wrinkles around their eyes contradicted the smooth flesh bursting from their tight costumes. Each time one of the women bent to set a tray of drinks on a table, her short leather skirt rode high to reveal the tops of her stockings. Depending on the woman's mood—and who perpetrated the act—the waitress jumped and giggled, or drew back and cursed whenever one of the men's hands caressed her thigh.

Bolan watched, his trained eyes picking up each detail, his disciplined brain recording the facts for future reference. The Golden Scorpion was a place where a man didn't blink his eyes. If he did, he was likely to find his wallet missing when he opened them.

He might also find a knife in his ribs.

Cool, dank night air hit the back of Bolan's neck as the door behind him opened. He glanced into the mirror and saw the two men enter the bar from the street.

The raucous laughter and loud conversations lowered to nervous snorts and whispers.

Bolan took another sip of beer as the two men crossed the room to a corner table. Slowly the noise level in the Golden Scorpion returned to normal.

The Executioner placed the beer bottle back on the bar. He studied the two men in the dim lighting. The older man looked to be about fifty. Even in the near darkness, he wore wire-rimmed aviator sunglasses. His thinning hair had been rinsed black except for a few strands of gray around the temples. He wore an olive green safari jacket and matching slacks. Still in good shape, he stood close to six feet tall. One-eighty, maybe one-eighty-five. In the shadows of the overhead lights, Bolan could see the man's pock-scarred face.

Gus Webster.

The other man, about six-two and as broad as a freight train, wore a fixed smile. Blond hair fell like a waterfall past his shoulders, down his back. Combined with his smooth, light skin and immense physique, the hair gave him the countenance of an ancient Norse god. He wore his calf-length, sailcloth duster unsnapped, revealing a black sport shirt and slacks. Bolan knew from Stony Man Farm intelligence what the long coat concealed—a Dan Wesson Super Mag and speedloaders carrying extra .357 Maximum rounds. The "Maxes" were more rifle than revolver cartridge. They'd leave the Super Mag's ten-and-a-half-inch barrel at a devastating 1,825 feet per second, boring through whatever they encountered like a diamond auger.

But the Super Mag was used only when long-range mayhem became necessary. For up-close work, the man in the long coat preferred a more basic, primitive weapon. Hanging from his belt opposite the revolver would be a Viking battle-ax with a five-inch "bearded" edge.

The man's name: Hugo Ulrikson.

Bolan held the beer bottle to his lips, then set it back on the bar next to the empty.

It was time to go to work.

The Executioner stood up, glanced around the room and started toward the hall leading to the rest room. As he passed the French sailors, the man with the wispy mustache scooted suddenly back. His chair rammed into the Executioner's thigh.

Bolan stopped. "Excuse me," he said and started to walk on.

The Frenchman rose quickly, grabbing his arm. "You are clumsy," he snarled in heavily accented English.

The warrior looked down at the smaller man. "I said excuse me."

"You Americans are all alike," the sailor growled. "You believe the world is yours. You may come and go as you please, run over whoever suits you." He paused, and a wicked grin sent the thin mustache hairs curling upward. Without warning, his fist flew toward Bolan's jaw.

The Executioner took a half step to the side, letting the punch pass harmlessly by his head. A right cross cracked into the sailor's chin, and he fell to the floor unconscious.

Bolan had started toward the rest room when he heard the voice behind him. "Perhaps you would care to try that with me, *monsieur.*"

The Executioner pivoted to see a tall sailor circle toward him from the other side of the table. The man stopped in front of Bolan and stared at him. Then his hand disappeared behind his back.

Bolan heard several clicking sounds, and the sailor's hand flew back into sight, the open blade of a Navaja ratchet knife extended from his fingers.

The Frenchman grinned, then lunged.

Bolan blocked the thrust, pushing the blade aside. He caught the wrist above the knife and pulled the man toward him as his other fist crashed into the sailor's face.

Blood shot from the Frenchman's nostrils. Bolan held on to the wrist as the sailor's head flew back, snapping like a whip.

Bolan threw a short uppercut into the knifer's sternum, and air rushed from the guy's lungs. He slumped to a sitting position on the floor, then fell backward, his head cracking against the cold concrete like a rifle shot.

The knife fell from his hand and skipped under a table.

The Executioner stepped back as the rest of the Frenchmen rose to their feet. A chubby man with a bandanna tied around his head reached under his shirt, the butt of a small-caliber automatic glistening from his belt.

Bolan's hand disappeared under the tail of his own shirt.

The small gun was halfway out of the fleshy sailor's belt when Bolan fired, the big Desert Eagle .44 Magnum bucking twice in his fist.

Blood burst from the sailor's chest and abdomen.

A Frenchman sporting long sideburns pulled a revolver from the top of his boot. Bolan squeezed the trigger again, and the man was kicked backward by the blast, the front of his T-shirt covered with crimson.

The Executioner backed slowly toward the door as the rest of the men at the table froze in their tracks. He kept the big .44 trained in their direction as he reached behind him and found the knob.

From the corner of his eye, he watched Gus Webster and Hugo Ulrikson. The two men sat calmly at the dark table in the corner, watching the show.

Both looked interested.

THE DOCK AREA was alive with drunks, thieves, con men and hookers as Bolan walked along the sidewalk toward the center of the city. At the first corner he turned to his right, pressed his back against the wall and peered back down the block toward the Golden Scorpion.

Hugo Ulrikson stepped onto the sidewalk.

Bolan ducked back and continued down the street, taking advantage of the opportunity to review what he knew about Ulrikson. The man had grown up in Helsingborg, in southern Sweden. A stone's throw across the water from Copenhagen, the natives of the area grew up more Danish than Swedish, and it was to Copenhagen that Ulrikson had eventually migrated.

The big Swede had been the Danish national judo champion four years running before joining NATO forces and seeing action on Cyprus. Returning to his home country, Ulrikson had served with the Swedish national police in Stockholm for less than a year before being dismissed.

Too many prisoners arrested by Ulrikson had arrived in court with bruises, broken bones ... or not at all.

The man hadn't stayed unemployed long, this time finding work more suitable to his disposition. He'd hit the mercenary trail, eventually becoming Gus Webster's right-hand man.

The denizens of the night were behind as Bolan entered a dense residential area. A routine scan of the international arms trade by Aaron "The Bear" Kurtzman, the computer wizard of Stony Man Farm's intel section, had kicked out four interesting facts.

First, a shipment of five hundred full-auto, Belgian-made Browning Hi-Power assault pistols had been sold by Fabrique Nationale a few months ago. The buyer: a Belize-based company known as Advance-Tech Arms. The sale had included wooden shoulder stocks and 100-round "snail drum" magazines for each weapon.

Second, Advance-Tech had purchased close to two thousand fragmentation grenades and a large supply of detonators and C-4 plastic explosive a week later.

Neither item by itself was mysterious. Purchasing weapons was what arms dealers did. It was facts three and four that had caused Kurtzman to contact the Executioner.

Three: none of the grenades, Hi-Powers, or C-4 had been resold by Advance-Tech.

And four: Raymond "Gus" Webster was the owner and CEO of Advance-Tech Arms, Inc.

Bolan continued through the residential area, passing three- and four-story luxury houses crammed together like American storefronts. Webster had a file with Interpol as thick as a power-lifter's thigh, but no convictions. For years the CIA, Justice Department and top police forces throughout the world had worked overtime trying to make something stick on the man. Using Advance-Tech as his cover, Webster had supplied arms to terrorists, dictators and anyone else willing to pay the price. And if the need was there, and the price was right, the Advance-Tech CEO was rumored to even recruit mercenaries who'd do the job.

All this was known to the law-enforcement agencies of the world. But knowing what the man did was one thing. Proving it in court was another. At least to most people.

Not the Executioner.

Bolan entered the business area of town, passing shops and stores with signs in French, Dutch and English. He turned down a side street to another series of bars and clubs. Drunks and scantily dressed women appeared, and the aura of depravity that had pervaded the dock-area dives returned.

The Executioner stopped at the next corner and looked over his shoulder. Ulrikson was still with him.

Bolan slowed his pace and stopped in front of a flashing neon sign announcing Le Rôtisserie. Loud music drifted through the open door. Onstage at the far end of the room, a woman wearing nothing but a lacy corset and a smirk gyrated to the beat.

Ulrikson rounded the corner and stopped dead.

Bolan turned, staring openly at the man. Then, confident that the big Swede knew he'd been spotted, the Executioner walked into the club, pushed aside a curtain at the side of the stage and entered a narrow, musky hall. He moved swiftly under the naked light bulb in the ceiling past an open door. Inside the dressing room, women in varying stages of dress sat in front of a dirty mirror. They looked up dispassionately as the warrior appeared.

Bolan pushed through a steel fire door at the end of the hall and stepped into the alley. He glanced both ways, pretending to overlook the shadowy figure in the long coat behind a trash bin. Chuckling softly, he made sure the sound was loud enough for Ulrikson to hear. Then, whistling, he turned away from the Swede and made his way down the alley back to the street.

Ten minutes later, the Executioner came to a row of specialty shops. Passing a sign that read Dagmar's Exotic Antiques and Jewels he circled the block twice, then cut between the buildings into the alley. A cat hissed, and tiny paws scampered past him as he crept toward the door behind the shop.

The Executioner pulled a lock pick from a pocket and went to work. As soon as the tumblers had fallen into line, he switched off his penflash, drew the Desert Eagle and turned for a final scan of the alley.

The shadow of a long coat fell into the alley by the entrance to the street.

Bolan slipped through the door and closed it behind him. Quickly moving to the jewelry section, he began filling a plastic sack with rings, watches and other small items of value, glancing at the wires running along the wall near the ceiling as he worked. A silent alarm. He had four minutes.

When the sack was full, Bolan shoved it under his jacket and returned to the back door. With the Desert Eagle leading the way, he stepped into the alley and closed the door.

As he reached the street, the Executioner saw the first police car racing toward Dagmar's. He crossed into the alley on the other side and continued past the cans and scattered trash.

Behind him, he could hear Ulrikson keeping pace.

Four blocks from Dagmar's, Bolan slowed to a brisk walk. He circled back toward the docks, keeping to the alleys and shadows. When a dilapidated rooming house appeared, he turned a full circle, his hand inside his jacket on the grips of the .44.

Hugo Ulrikson was nowhere to be seen.

The Executioner pulled the key from his pocket and mounted the front steps of the rooming house. Inside, he climbed another rickety staircase to the second floor, then opened the door to Room Number Six.

Keeping the lights off, the warrior dropped the sack of jewelry on the tattered bedspread and crossed the room to the window. Drawing the curtain cautiously to the side, he looked outside.

Hugo Ulrikson stood across the street staring up at the rooming house.

Bolan closed the curtain, switched on the light and sat on the bed. He drew the Desert Eagle from his waistband, dropped the magazine and worked the slide to eject the chambered round.

A short, leadless brass casing fell onto the pillow.

The Executioner slid his suitcase from under the bed. He pulled a fresh magazine of live .44 Magnum from the flap pocket in the divider, and rammed it up the well of the Desert Eagle, replacing the blanks.

A hard smile formed on Bolan's face. The American agents posing as French sailors had done their jobs well. Even the remote-controlled blood packs hidden beneath their clothing had been timed perfectly.

Bolan's mind returned to Webster and Ulrikson. Five hundred full-auto assault pistols. Two thousand frags. Plastique.

What did it all mean? He didn't know. The smile on the Executioner's lips faded and was replaced with a frown of determination.

He didn't know, but he'd find out.

Bolan worked the slide of the Desert Eagle, jacking a .44 Magnum hollowpoint into the chamber.

Playtime was over. From here on in, it would be live ammo all the way.

FOOTSTEPS SOUNDED in the hall.

Bolan opened his eyes. The first rays of early morning radiated through the flimsy curtains. He rose from the bed, stuffed the pillows under the blanket and jerked the spread to the headboard.

Metal scratched against metal as a key slid into the lock.

Bolan snatched the Desert Eagle from the nightstand and moved behind the door. His back against the peeling wallpaper, he waited as the bolt clicked and the knob twisted.

The door eased slowly open.

Hugo Ulrikson edged into the room and moved cautiously to the bed. The big Swede gripped a Dan Wesson Super Mag in his right hand, the ten-inch barrel aimed at the lump beneath the bedspread. He shoved the heavy barrel into the pillows.

"Wake up," he ordered in a low, gravelly voice.

The Executioner stepped behind him and dug the Desert Eagle into his spine. "I'm up. Don't move or *you* won't be." Swiftly he reached around the Swede and jerked the Super Mag from his hand.

Bolan moved to the wall and flipped on the light. "Turn around."

As Ulrikson turned, he wore the same fixed smile the Executioner had seen on his face in the Golden Scorpion. But behind it, in the eyes, Bolan saw the fury that surged through the giant's soul.

"Before I kill you," the warrior said, "do you want to tell me what you came for?"

The smile didn't falter. "A man wants to see you."

Bolan snorted and shook his head. "Friend, there's a lot of men who would like to see me. Some have tried. A few got a decent burial, but most are rotting away in the remote corners of the world." He paused, then said, "You're about to join them."

The big Swede shook his head and slowly held up his hands, palms out. "No. This man wants to offer you a job."

Bolan stared at him. Things were going as planned. Almost too well. He glanced briefly to Ulrikson's side where he knew the battle-ax was concealed, and reminded himself to stay wary of the beaming face.

"What man are you talking about?"

The Swede's smile widened. "Gus Webster."

Bolan shrugged. "I don't know any Gus Webster, and I don't need a job."

This time it was Ulrikson who snorted in contempt. "Let's quit playing games, Giddings," he said, using Bolan's cover name. "Everyone knows who Gus Webster is. Especially anyone who goes into the Golden Scorpion. And if you don't need money, why did you waste your time on that penny-ante burglary last night?"

Bolan shifted the Desert Eagle slightly, tilting the barrel in line with the smiling face. He lowered his eyebrows, letting his face twist into feigned surprise. "How do you know my name?"

Ulrikson chuckled. "It's a simple enough procedure to check the register downstairs, Mr. Al Giddings. Yes, yes, I know the management here is famous for never exposing their boarders." He laughed again, then tapped his side. "But I can be very persuasive when I choose to be." He held up the key in his hand. "They were quite cooperative."

Bolan glanced toward the sack of jewelry on the table. "How'd you know about that?"

"You're not quite as good at losing tails as you think you are. Personally I doubt if you're as good at anything as you think." The big Swede shrugged his shoulders. "But Mr. Webster was impressed with you last night, so here I am." He paused and drew in a deep breath. "I've been patient with you, Mr. Giddings. But now I suggest you return my weapon and put your own away before you get hurt.'' The smile remained intact through the threat.

Bolan grinned back. It was time to establish the pecking order. If not, Ulrikson would think he had the upper hand. The Executioner was certain to be spending at least *some* time with this overgrown bully during the next few days, and he didn't intend to do it in a subservient position.

He dropped the Desert Eagle onto the bed and transferred the Super Mag to his right hand. "Think you can take me?'' he asked.

"I have no doubt.''

Slowly Bolan swung the cylinder out of the mammoth revolver and dropped the long .357 Maximum cartridges to the floor. He tossed the massive gun to the corner of the room. "Let's find out.''

Ulrikson continued to smile as he circled to his right, crouching slightly, shuffling in traditional judo movements. "I should warn you, Giddings,'' he said. "I was the Scandinavian judo champion for years. I retired undefeated.''

Bolan stepped in, and the big Swede reached for him.

The Executioner's right leg shot out, catching Ulrikson in the knee. A low, hoarse moan escaped the man's lips, which was silenced with a left hook to the jaw.

Ulrikson sprawled back across the bed, reaching under his duster for the battle-ax.

Bolan grabbed the Beretta 93-R from the nightstand and took a step back as the battle-ax appeared in Ulrikson's hand. The Executioner pointed to the ax with the Beretta's barrel. "I don't know the rules of judo, but I'm pretty sure that's cheating." He leveled the Beretta at his opponent's nose. "Now, drop the hatchet."

The smile on Ulrikson's face finally vanished as the ax fell to the bed.

Bolan watched him as hatred, pure and simple, replaced the smile. Then the fixed grin slowly returned.

The Executioner shoved the Beretta into his belt. For the time being, it was over. But he had no doubt that this was only Round One. Hugo Ulrikson wasn't used to being defeated, and he didn't like it. Sooner or later, the man would have to try him again.

Bolan walked to the corner of the room and picked up the Super Mag. He flipped it end over end to Ulrikson, who snatched it out of the air.

"Stick your toys back under your coat," the Executioner said. He stared Ulrikson in the eye. "Then we'll go see this guy named Webster."

THE SUN SHONE directly overhead, its warm rays burning down through the brisk spring air of Limburg province in eastern Belgium.

Thick green pine trees formed a near-solid wall on both sides of the highway. Between the forest and the road, wildflowers of every size, shape, texture and hue formed a tunnel of color for the Lincoln Mark IV to pass through.

Bolan glanced at the road sign as Ulrikson turned the car off the highway onto the gravel—Hasselt 8 kilometers.

The big Swede guided the Lincoln through a series of curves until an iron gate appeared in the distance. The vehicle slowed.

A man clad in green fatigues stepped from a guard shack just past the gate, an FN LAR rifle cradled in his arms. His eyebrows rose slightly as he recognized the car. Scampering back into the shack, he pressed a button. A moment later, the gate swung open.

The luxury car continued down the road, and as Ulrikson rounded a curve, a Swiss-chalet-style house came into view.

"We're here," the big Swede announced.

Bolan remained silent as they stepped out of the car. He scanned the premises, instinctively registering cover, concealment and avenues of escape if worse came to worst. The Executioner didn't expect any trouble at this juncture of the mission. It was too early. But he hadn't survived countless battles in the hell-grounds by being careless.

A servant wearing a short white jacket met them at the front door. "Ah, Mr. Ulrikson."

Ulrikson nodded. "Jean-Marc."

"Mr. Webster is waiting by the pond." Jean-Marc turned and led Bolan and Ulrikson down the hall. They passed through an enormous reception room and into an equally large kitchen. The servant opened the back door and turned to face them. "Please inform Mr. Webster that lunch will be ready in half an hour."

Ulrikson nodded again as Jean-Marc hurried away, then he led Bolan out the door onto a large patio.

A white cast-iron table and matching chairs sat in the shade under a large umbrella. Bolan followed Ulrikson onto a walkway, and carefully manicured evergreen shrubs. A row of thickly branched pines encircled the shrubs, secluding the patio from outside view.

The walk twisted through the shrubs and trees, suddenly opening onto a large clearing in the forest. Fifty yards in the distance, just before the heavy woods started again, was a pond.

Gus Webster stood next to the water, facing away from the house. The CEO of Advance-Tech Arms wore bleached white Gurkha shorts and a matching shirt with epaulets on the shoulders. A Browning BDA .38 protruded from the top of his shorts.

Webster drew a fly rod back over his shoulder and cast a black-and-yellow lure to the middle of the pond.

Ulrikson stopped Bolan twenty yards away. "Never sneak up on the man," he said. "It's a damn good way to get shot." He cleared his throat loudly. "Gus?"

Webster turned to face them. He smiled below the sunglasses, the pockmarks on his face standing out in bold relief under the midday sun. "Ah, Mr. Giddings." Webster began reeling in the line as the new arrivals moved toward him.

Bolan and Ulrikson waited while Webster hooked the lure into the rod's cork grip, then dropped it to the ground. He turned to the Swede. "Let's have a drink before lunch." He extended his hand, indicating the path back to the house. "Shall we?"

The Executioner followed the two men back through the bushes and flowers to the patio, where they took seats around the cast-iron table.

Jean-Marc seemed to materialize out of thin air. "What will you have, Mr. Webster?"

Webster turned his eyes to the sky and frowned, as if this might be his most important decision of the day. "Dry sherry, I think," he finally said. "With a cherry...no, let's make it an olive."

"Very good, sir." He turned to Ulrikson. "And the usual Jagermeister for you, sir?"

Ulrikson nodded.

Webster laughed and turned to Bolan. "As you can see, Mr. Giddings, class doesn't necessarily follow wealth. While Hugo has grown rich in my employ, I've never been able to break him of the nasty habit of confusing cordials with aperitifs. Jagermeister." The word came out of his mouth as if it tasted bad. "Hugo would drink that root-beer-flavored gorilla urine for breakfast, given the chance." He turned to Ulrikson. "Sweet drinks before dinner stifle the appetite, Hugo."

The Swede shrugged the duster from his shoulders, hung it over the back of his chair, then rolled the sleeves of his shirt up on his arms. Curling his wrists, he flexed his massive biceps, causing tiny veins to bulge beneath the skin. "Does it look like I'm suffering from malnutrition, Gus?" he asked, the plastic smile never leaving his face.

The arms dealer laughed. Jean-Marc coughed impatiently.

Webster turned to his servant. "Don't get bitchy now, Jean-Marc." To Bolan, he said, "Jean-Marc is anxious to know what you'll have, Mr. Giddings."

"A beer will be fine."

"Heineken? St Pauli Girl? Grolsch? We probably have whatever you like."

"Stella's fine."

Jean-Marc disappeared into the kitchen. Webster pulled a gold cigarette case from the pocket of his shorts. Flipping the latch, he offered it to Bolan.

Bolan shook his head.

"Pity. These are the finest Turkish—"

Bolan cut in on him. "I don't smoke, Webster, and I don't waste time, either. What am I here for?"

Both Webster's and Ulrikson's eyes shot up in surprise. It was clear the Advance-Tech CEO wasn't used to being talked to in that fashion.

The Executioner waited.

Webster opened his mouth to speak, but Jean-Marc reappeared. The servant placed their drinks before them, then set a bowl of raw vegetables and dip on the table before returning to the kitchen.

The arms dealer sipped his sherry. He held the glass by the stem as he spoke. "So, Mr. Giddings, you're like Hugo, eh? Not one for formalities. No time for small talk or the finer things of life? No matter. Sometimes they're merely distractions—distractions that cannot be afforded." He took another sip of his drink. "We'll discuss the details over lunch, but basically you're here because I was impressed with your performance last night at the Golden Scorpion. I can use a man with your talents." He paused, staring Bolan in the eye. "If you can be trusted. Can I trust you, Mr. Giddings?"

Bolan stared back. "Within reason."

Webster chuckled softly. "An honest answer. I like that. Tell me about yourself."

The warrior shook his head. "Why should *I* trust *you?*"

"Touché. It seems we're at a standoff."

Jean-Marc stuck his head out the door. "Lunch is served, sir."

Webster and Ulrikson rose to their feet. Bolan followed them through the door and down the hall to an elaborately decorated dining room. A crystal chandelier hung from the ceiling over a long mahogany dining table. The table had been set with china, silver, and salt and pepper shakers that matched the chandelier.

Webster took a seat at the head of the table, indicating that Ulrikson should sit on his right, Bolan on his left.

"I believe I have a place for you within my organization," he began.

"And what makes you think I'm interested?" Bolan asked.

"Hugo informs me that you broke into a—what was it?—an antique store last night. Stole some jewelry?" He paused as a maid entered the room and set plates of scampi in front of them.

After the woman left, Webster continued. "For a man of your abilities, that was a foolish act, Mr. Giddings. The act of someone desperate for money."

Bolan didn't answer.

The men fell silent as they ate their appetizer. When they'd finished, the maid collected the plates while Jean-Marc appeared with fresh wineglasses and a bottle of red Pomeral.

As the servant filled their glasses, the woman returned with the main course.

"Mr. Giddings," Webster said, waving his hand before him, indicating the room. "What you see before you is only the beginning. I have plans for... 'expansion,' I suppose we should call it." He grinned at Ulrikson and the big Swede winked. Turning back to Bolan, he said, "Plans beyond your wildest dreams, Mr. Giddings. And you could be part of them."

Bolan stared back at him. "Let's say I'm interested. What do I do, and how much do I get paid?"

Webster sliced daintily at his meat with a bone-handled steak knife. He chewed thoughtfully and dabbed his lips with a linen napkin before answering. "A thousand dollars a day when you work, Mr. Giddings. That will go up after you've proved yourself. But exactly what you'll be required to do, I can't say." The Advance-Tech CEO shrugged. "It depends on what needs to be done."

"Let's give it a try," the Executioner said.

Webster nodded in satisfaction.

The men finished their meals. Webster rang a small bell to summon Jean-Marc. "Please usher in Deetlev, Jean-Marc."

A few moments later a short, stocky man with a high forehead walked through the door. He nodded to Ulrikson and stopped next to Webster.

"Mr. Giddings . . . Mr. Deetlev Van Doorn," Webster said.

"Deetlev, take Mr. Giddings to Antwerp with you. He's entering a probationary period with Advance-

Tech, and I want you to watch him closely." The CEO's voice trailed off as he took a sip of wine.

"Stay off the booze, Deetlev. When you return with your report, I'll decide if our new friend can be trusted. Or if he should be killed."

2

Gus Webster watched Giddings and Van Doorn file out of the room. He turned to Ulrikson.

"Give me your impression of Mr. Giddings."

"Easy. I don't like him, Gus, and I don't trust him."

Webster nodded. "Yes. I could tell that the moment you walked in. Distrust is understandable, under the circumstances. We know very little about him. But could your resentment stem at all from the new bruise on your face?" He watched the Swede's skin turn red around the bruise.

"He caught me off guard."

Jean-Marc entered the room and placed a brandy snifter in front of his boss and a Jagermeister in front of Ulrikson. The Advance-Tech CEO chose a long, thick Havana cigar from the wooden humidor and lighted it with a slim gold lighter. He lifted the snifter by the stem and let the aroma of fermented pears fill his nostrils.

Webster raised the snifter into the air and waited while Ulrikson did the same with his shot glass of Jagermeister. "To us, Hugo," he said. "Business as it is, it's so infrequent that we see each other anymore."

Ulrikson nodded. They drank.

Webster inhaled a lungful of the rich Cuban tobacco. Smoke trailed out his nose and mouth as he
spoke. "What concerns me, old friend, is the man's
unwillingness to disclose anything about his past. Give
references, if you will. Perhaps he is what he infers to
us—a wanted man on the run, unwilling to trust anyone. But that would be a convenient cover for a law-
enforcement officer, as well."

Ulrikson shook his head. "He's no cop. *I* was a cop.
I know what they can do, and what they can't. Giddings killed two sailors in the Scorpion, and I saw him
pull a burglary with my own eyes." The big Swede
paused and downed the remainder of his drink. "No
cop is going to do that."

Webster laughed. "You're so competent at times,
Hugo. At other times, you can be so naive. You and I
both come from civilized countries where such things
are forbidden by law. But we must remember that in
many parts of the world, most parts actually, that isn't
the case." He pulled a silver ashtray toward him and
carefully rolled the end of his cigar. "And I have no
doubt that certain factions within the CIA would
consider a few unruly French sailors expendable."

Webster finished his brandy, letting the last of the
pear-flavored fire linger in his mouth before it slid
down his throat. He glanced at Ulrikson, saw the
concern on the big Swede's face and realized suddenly that the man was afraid.

Giddings had gotten the better of him. Hugo Ulrikson had seen the man's capabilities up close and
personal, and feared Giddings might be better than
him.

Ulrikson feared he might be replaced.

Webster chuckled inwardly. A little competition would be good for the big Swede. Keep him on his toes. And in any case, Advance-Tech could use two good commanders—especially for his expansion plans.

"Hugo, the fingerprints from Mr. Giddings's glasses and utensils. Lift them, then run them through our police contact in Brussels. If Giddings is a spy of some type, we'll find out. And if he's wanted like he says, then we'll have just that much more to hang over his head. Let's go for a walk."

As they reached the trees and started down a narrow path, Ulrikson said, "Gus, I see no reason to gamble. If there's a chance at all that he's a cop, or an agent, why not just kill him and get it over with? Van Doorn can help me with—"

"No," Webster said, cutting him off. "As you're well aware, Deetlev is quite excellent at what he does. But he has his—what should we call them—peculiarities? Yes, and those same peculiarities that make him valuable create certain limitations."

"So why put up with the drunken sot at all?" Ulrikson growled. "We have other men capable of the same things he does."

Webster shook his head. "You know the answer to that, Hugo. He saved my life." He felt the familiar burn in his abdomen. His hand found its way under his shirt to the seasoned bullet scar.

"You've paid him back a thousandfold."

"Yes, perhaps you're right." Webster sighed. He continued to rub the old wound. "But in any case,

Deetlev or anyone else in my employment is incapable of overseeing things as you do. But Giddings might be able to." He watched the Swede from the corner of his eye. Ulrikson's face reddened again.

Webster patted the taller man on the shoulder. "Relax, Hugo," he said. "You have been an excellent right-hand man. But our operations have grown even faster than I imagined, and for what we have planned, I need a left hand as well."

"Then at least let me bring in Duggan," Ulrikson urged. "In case Giddings doesn't work out. That way I'll have someone I trust to help me keep an eye on him."

Webster stopped in his tracks. He took another puff of the cigar and stared at the sky. "Yes. An excellent idea, Hugo." He patted the big Swede's shoulder again. "Do that. We must be prepared for all contingencies. And even if Giddings does work out, your IRA friend can be used in the upcoming operation."

DUSK HAD FALLEN by the time Bolan and Deetlev Van Doorn reached the port city of Antwerp. The Executioner had been subjected to the man's nonstop, machine-gun chatter since leaving Webster's country house. He'd rambled endlessly about his feats, both with women and in combat with the South African Reconnaissance Commandos.

Had Bolan taken Van Doorn's boasts at face value, he'd have been convinced that the man was a flawless cross between Rambo and Don Juan.

The Executioner had learned a lot about Van Doorn but little about Advance-Tech's operation as a whole.

He still had no idea what Webster's "expansion" plans might be. As for their purpose in Antwerp, the Executioner had been told only that they were about to purchase a million rounds of 9 mm ammunition from Israeli Military Industries.

Bolan turned in his seat to face Van Doorn as the man guided the Lincoln down the winding streets of the city toward the docks. The South African wore a light, unlined sport coat, rolled up over his hairy forearms. The jacket hid two weapons: a Tanarmi 9 mm automatic and a long Chris Reeve Jereboam survival knife.

He turned back to the windshield. Van Doorn was a braggart, a liar, and if the broken veins around his nose were any indication, one hell of a heavy drinker. Whatever part he played in the Advance-Tech operation, it had to be minimal. But Bolan needed to learn all the man knew. And if the only info the South African planned to offer concerned his own escapades, then the warrior would have to get the ball rolling himself.

The Executioner took a deep breath. "Where'd you meet Webster?" he asked offhandedly.

Van Doorn turned to him. "Saved his life, that's how."

"Is that right."

"Damn straight it is. Pulled him right out of the jungle with a bullet in his gut."

"Where?"

Van Doorn frowned. "I'm supposed to watch you, mate, find out about *you*. Not tell you about *us*."

Bolan shrugged. "Just making conversation."

"Guess it can't hurt any. Rhodesia, 1974. I was with the South African Recce Commandos. Did I tell you that before?"

"A time or two." The sarcasm passed over Van Doorn's head.

"Webster was running a merc squad that fought alongside us for a while."

"Ulrikson with him?"

"Nah," Van Doorn said. "The Swede showed up after he got kicked out of the Swedish cops or something. Me and Webster were both in Angola by then. Anyways, Webster always had big ideas. Convinced me I could do better with him than in the army, and still do what I liked for a living."

"What's that?"

Van Doorn turned to him, his eyebrows rising as if he'd just been asked what planet he was from. "Why, kill kaffirs, mate. Kill bloody kaffirs."

Bolan felt his blood boil at the term. It was the South African equivalent of "nigger"—an insult to blacks in general, and particularly to the many fine black soldiers who had fought next to the Executioner over the years.

Van Doorn turned a corner, and the docks appeared in the distance. They continued down the cobbled street, past bars and warehouses until they reached the quayside. The South African pulled the vehicle to a halt as an old man wearing a Greek fisherman's cap walked toward them, a pack slung over his back.

Van Doorn rolled down his window. "Looking for an Israeli vessel, mate," he said in Flemish as the old man bent toward him. "Seen it docked?"

Dirty gray hair peeked from under his cap as the old man's head bobbed up and down. "Aye." He then gave directions in what Bolan recognized as the Brabant dialect.

Van Doorn threw the Lincoln back in drive and they cruised slowly along the canal leading to the North Sea.

Bolan turned to him again. "Where are we taking the ammo?"

"That's for me to know, mate. Webster don't trust you yet."

A few minutes later, a worked-over American Liberty ship appeared in the distance. The markings on the hull came into focus as the Lincoln drew alongside the bow—*King David*.

Van Doorn parked the car and they walked down the steps toward the freighter.

A dark-skinned man in a blue chambray shirt appeared on deck at the bow of the ship. He looked over the hull, and the smile on his face disappeared. "Ah, Deetlev Van Doorn," he called down in Israeli-accented English. "What good fortune to see you again," he added with just a trace of sarcasm.

The South African looked up and nodded, oblivious to the man's attitude. "Where the hell's our ship, Isaac?"

"She radioed in a half hour ago. Delayed last night at Dover...engine trouble. She'll dock in the morning."

"Bloody hell," Van Doorn spit. Then a strange grin lighted up his face. He turned to Bolan. "Well, mate, we'll be staying over, then. Have to supervise the exchange—make sure we're not cheated, you know."

The two men climbed the steps back to the car as the sun finally fell over the horizon.

"Time for a little fun, mate." Van Doorn turned the car away from the water and pulled away from the docks.

The Antwerp wharf area looked no different than that surrounding the Golden Scorpion in Ostend. Women in short leather skirts and too much makeup stood on street corners, propositioning the drunken sailors who stumbled in and out of the bars. As they moved down the trash-littered streets, Bolan watched a boy of thirteen skillfully dip his hand into the back pocket of a passing merchant marine. He came up with a wallet, turned quickly and passed it off to another boy. The second kid stuffed the prize between the folds of a newspaper and walked away.

Van Doorn finally pulled to a halt in front of a red neon sign announcing Le Rouge. He led Bolan across the sidewalk, down a cracked concrete staircase and into the club.

Thick cigarette smoke rose to the ceiling as they pushed through the door. On the stage at the end of the room, a heavy-metal band blasted away, threatening to crack the plaster on the walls. The Executioner glanced up at a sign over the bar. The Belgian health authorities had authorized the club to hold no more than eighty people at one time. There had to be at least two hundred drunken, sweating bodies gyrating on the dance floor. More if you counted those crammed together at the bar and tables.

Bolan followed Van Doorn to a table next to the dance floor. Two young men, wearing the insignia of Dutch ensigns, sat staring straight ahead as if in comas. Empty bottles and shot glasses littered their table. Others had fallen to the floor.

The new arrivals stopped in front of the table just as one of the Dutchmen gave up the fight and slumped face-first to the floor. Van Doorn hooked a foot under his ribs, jostled him out of the way and took his seat. The South African reached out, stuck a hand across the table to the other man's face and shoved. The Dutchman joined his friend on the floor and Bolan was motioned to the chair.

Van Doorn swept the bottles and glasses from the table with a thick forearm. They crashed to the floor as a weary, middle-aged waitress strutted forward. She wore either a short dress or a wide belt—Bolan wasn't sure which. Flaming red hair fell to her shoulders, and her makeup had cracked like a long-dry creek bed. Bolan watched her eyes flicker over the Dutch sailors on the floor.

The woman took their orders and disappeared through the crowd as the band suddenly quieted and went into a series of slow dances.

Van Doorn leaned across the table. "A drink or two, mate," he shouted at Bolan, "then we go looking for some women." The South African winked lecherously.

The red-headed waitress returned. She set a shot of Geneva gin in front of Van Doorn and gave both men a Heineken beer. Van Doorn downed the gin in one gulp and grabbed her arm as she turned away. "Two more," he ordered.

The waitress rolled her eyes, picked up his glass and vanished once more into the throng.

Bolan sat back and sipped at his beer. He glanced at Van Doorn. The man had already guzzled most of his beer and was staring hungrily at the bumping bodies on the dance floor.

Bolan set his bottle on the table and continued to watch. The South African was one of the more unappealing human beings he'd come across in some time, but he'd have to put up with him for a while. At least if he wanted to find out what Webster had planned.

Van Doorn reached out and pinched a passing woman on the buttocks. The woman screamed.

The Executioner turned away. It was going to be a long night.

The South African downed five more shots of gin in the next thirty minutes, looking scornfully at Bolan each time the Executioner refused another round. Finally he leaned across the table and slurred, "Finish your beer—I'll be back."

Bolan watched him totter toward the dance floor.

Van Doorn returned five minutes later with two women in tow, surprising the warrior in more ways than one. One of the women wore stylish designer jeans and a white blouse open almost to the waist. The other had on a bright yellow dress with a slit up the side that went almost to her waist. The breasts of both women strained against their garments and bounced with each step that brought them closer to the table.

Their presence in a place like this could spell only one thing: pros. But what surprised the Executioner even more was the fact that the women were black.

Van Doorn and the women took seats around the table. The man then screamed over the music until the tired waitress took his order.

Bolan leaned in close to him so the women couldn't hear. "I thought you didn't like blacks," he whispered.

"I like the *cows.*"

The Executioner resisted the sudden urge to punch the man in the face. His eyes flickered toward the women, then back to Van Doorn. "I'm running a little low until Webster pays me. How much is this going to cost?"

Van Doorn waved a hand in front of his face. "Forget it. It's on the company." He paused long enough for another leering grin, then sat back and threw an arm around the neck of the woman in yellow. His hand disappeared into her exposed cleavage.

The woman in the white blouse turned to Bolan. She was eighteen, maybe twenty. But even in the darkness of the club, the Executioner could see the toll her trade was extracting—lines of dissatisfaction around her mouth, stress lines on her forehead. His eyes dropped automatically to her arms. The skin and veins on the inside of her elbows were pocked and ulcerated.

The young woman leaned forward, smiling. *"Parlez-vous français?"* she asked.

Bolan nodded. "A little."

"I'm Aziza," she said in French. "My friend is Mireille."

"Call me Al." Bolan looked across the table. Van Doorn might be drunk, but he was watching every move. The women were a test—a test to see how he responded.

Bolan smiled at Aziza and took a sip of his beer. He'd have to come up with something quick, unless he wanted to end up in a hotel room with Deetlev Van Doorn and these two women. But he couldn't make it look like he was unwilling. Not if he intended to be taken into Webster's inner circle.

The Executioner moved his chair closer to Aziza. From the corner of his eye, he saw Van Doorn's lecherous smirk.

Bolan and Aziza made small talk for the next hour, while Van Doorn inhaled another half-dozen shots and beers. When the band onstage finally called a halt, the South African rose unsteadily to his feet. "I'm ready," he bellowed to the entire club. He turned to Bolan. "You ready, mate?"

Bolan nodded. "Ready and willing." He leaned close to Aziza. "There's just one thing...."

Aziza's eyebrows narrowed.

"Never mind."

"No, please. Tell me," Aziza urged.

"No, really. I'm sure it won't make any difference."

The concern on the black woman's face mounted. "Please tell me what you were about to say."

"Well, I went to the doctor three days ago. He told me to stay clean. Don't do anything for two weeks."

The Executioner paused, letting it sink in. "But I can wear a condom. I've been taking the penicillin and the symptoms are gone. I'm sure you won't get it." He smiled. "You ready?" He stood and extended his hand.

The young black woman shrank from the hand as if it were a snake. She hurried to Mireille's side and whispered into the other woman's ear.

Mireille stared at Bolan and nodded.

Aziza smiled nervously back to the Executioner, then hurried across the dance floor, up the steps and out of the bar.

BOLAN DROPPED his suitcase to the floor, closed the door behind him, turned and surveyed the hotel room. Paper peeled from the walls; a broken mirror hung over the bureau; a splintered table was propped in the corner.

The mattress was too long for the bed. It had been jammed into the frame at both foot and head, causing it to fold in the middle.

In the hall, Bolan heard Mireille's tipsy laughter and Van Doorn's drunken cackle. The metal shrieked like chalk on a blackboard as the South African fumbled to get his key in the lock next door. "Bloody fuckin' hell!" he roared in frustration.

Bolan dropped his jacket on the chair and slid out of the shoulder holster. He hung the Beretta over the bedpost next to his pillow. The Desert Eagle came next, finding a resting spot on top of the bureau.

The Executioner dropped to a seat on the bed as Van Doorn's door finally opened.

The warrior lay back and clasped his hands behind his head as the bedsprings in the next room began to creak. The mattress bridged his back into an uncomfortable position, and combined with the noise, he wasn't likely to get much sleep.

On the other side of the thin wall, Mireille began to moan. Van Doorn's boorish laughter penetrated the plaster. "You like that, do you?" he grunted.

Bolan's eyes closed tighter in an attempt to shut it out. He'd had enough of this. He had to find a way to speed things along, make Webster trust him enough to reveal what he'd planned.

Mireille's moans turned to loud pants. Suddenly a shrill shriek pierced the walls.

The Executioner bounded to his feet, his hand grasping the butt of the Beretta in the shoulder rig on the bed post.

Another scream. Then, "Please! No!"

Bolan heard a dull thud as he ripped open the door to the hall. More thumps—knuckles on flesh—came through the door as he twisted the knob to the South African's room. Locked.

"Please!"

The Executioner took a step back and kicked at the lock. The rotting door flew off the hinges into the room. Bolan followed it inside.

Mireille lay nude, spread-eagled on the bed. Her wrists and ankles had been bound to the posts with brightly colored scarves.

Van Doorn was still dressed. He held the long blade of the survival knife to Mireille's throat with one hand, while his other fist pummeled her face, chest and ribs. "Bloody...fuckin'...bitch," he panted.

Bolan shoved the Beretta into his belt and crossed the room in two bounding steps. He grasped Van Doorn's knife hand at the wrist and twisted up and back.

The South African shrieked in both pain and surprise. "What do you—"

Bolan spun Van Doorn to face him, then delivered a short left jab to the man's jaw. The long survival blade fell to the floor.

The Executioner grabbed Van Doorn by the collar and dragged him from the bed as footsteps pounded down the hall.

An unshaved man in boxer shorts stuck his head into the room. "What's going on?"

A heartbeat later, an elderly woman in curlers joined him in the doorway. She stared in horrified fascination at Mireille.

"Get up," Bolan ordered Van Doorn, who'd collapsed to the floor.

The South African complied, rubbing his jaw.

The woman in curlers screamed as the shock wore off.

A younger man in a T-shirt joined the spectators. "Call the police," he ordered the woman in Flemish. She padded quickly back down the hall.

Bolan grabbed the survival knife and cut through the scarves around Mireille's hands and feet. He turned back to Van Doorn.

The South African's hand was under his jacket, a cold stare of hatred in his eyes.

The warrior stepped forward and kicked as Van Doorn drew the Tanarmi 9 mm pistol. The gun went flying across the room, and its owner fell back, holding his wrist.

"I said get up," Bolan told him. "Cops are on the way." He reached down, grasped Van Doorn under the arms and hauled him to his feet. Then he sprinted across the room, retrieved the Tanarmi and shoved it into his belt next to the Beretta. He handed the knife to Van Doorn. "Stick it in the sheath. Try to use it and I'll kill you."

Strains of fast-approaching sirens could be heard through the window.

Bolan grabbed Van Doorn with one hand, the man's suitcase with the other and hustled them both next door. Slipping into the rigs for the Beretta and Desert Eagle, he covered them with his jacket and grabbed his own travel bag.

"Give me my gun," Van Doorn demanded drunkenly. "We'll kill the bloody pigs if they—"

"Sure. Just the kind of heat we need." He shoved Van Doorn back into the hall, then half carried the drunken man down the stairs.

Blue uniforms appeared through the front windows of the hotel as the two men reached the ground floor. Still steering the South African, Bolan raced through the dining room and into the kitchen, surprising the help as they cleaned up for the night.

The door from the kitchen led to the alley. The Executioner pushed Van Doorn through first, then followed. They reached the corner and jogged to the parking lot. "Give me the keys," Bolan demanded.

Van Doorn reached into his pocket and obliged.

The warrior slid behind the wheel of the Lincoln, revving the engine to life as Van Doorn stumbled into the passenger seat.

The Executioner threw the vehicle into drive and pulled out of the parking lot. He glanced at Van Doorn. The man's face had turned a sallow, sickly color. He wished he didn't need the loathsome savage anymore. The man was a racist, a murderer and a sadist who preyed on the weak of the world.

But the Executioner would have to wait to kill him.

3

The sun peeked over the horizon, chasing the shadows of night from the dock as Bolan pulled to a halt. He turned to Van Doorn. The snoring lump lay half off the seat, his head tilted back, spittle hanging from the corners of his drooping lips.

Deetlev Van Doorn looked like a man who'd died several days ago—a long way from the nearest embalmer. He belched, and the stale odor of Dutch gin rose through the car. Bolan rolled down the window, letting the cool, early-morning breeze off the canal sweep into the vehicle.

Van Doorn belched again, then slowly opened his eyes. "Where are we?"

"At the docks," Bolan told him. He pointed to a medium-size coastal freighter tied up alongside the pier next to the Israeli ship. Bright red letters across the front of the hull announced it as the *Pegasus*. "Is that ours?"

Van Doorn straightened in the seat, squinting through the windshield with one hand cupped over his forehead. "Yeah." He groaned, slumped back in the seat and closed his eyes again.

Bolan reached over and shook his shoulder.

The South African's eyelids struggled back open. "What time is it?"

"Almost 0700. Let's go." Bolan opened the door and started down the steps to the pier. Behind him, he heard Van Doorn's belabored footsteps.

The Executioner glanced over his shoulder. So far, the man had given no signs that he even remembered last night's events. But as the day grew on and he sobered up, Van Doorn's memory was likely to return.

Bolan knew he'd have to stay on his toes, watch Van Doorn's mood, then explain his actions as best he could.

Dressed in crisp khaki uniforms, several of the *King David*'s crew stood on the pier, smoking, chatting and waiting to unload.

On the deck of the *Pegasus,* Bolan could see the motley men of the Advance-Tech ship. Wearing filthy work clothes and a variety of hats and caps, they looked like nothing so much as a band of over-the-hill, back-alley cutthroats.

Isaac stepped forward from the middle of the Israelis and walked to meet them. He looked past Bolan. "Ah, Deetlev," he said, his face a mixture of amusement and revulsion. "Another battle with the bottle? And again, it appears you have lost."

"Fuck you, Isaac. Let's get it over with."

Van Doorn stood unsteadily next to Bolan as Isaac boarded the *King David*. A few minutes later, a forklift came rolling down the docks and onto the Israeli ship. It descended a moment later loaded with boxes marked Israeli Military Industries.

As they supervised the unloading, Van Doorn's hangover changed from mere discomfort to shakes. Bolan watched as sweat broke out on the man's forehead. The South African began shifting his weight nervously from leg to leg, taking shallow breaths and massaging his temples with his fingertips. Finally he turned to Bolan. "Uh, listen, Giddings," he said. "I've got some other business to take care of. Think you can handle this alone?"

Bolan didn't answer.

Van Doorn glanced nervously up the street. "Just, uh, watch and count, and make sure they don't fuck us."

The warrior followed the South African's line of sight and saw a red-and-blue neon sign blinking off and on. The Purple Parrot. "You have any reason to think they'll cheat us?" he asked.

Van Doorn stared at him. "They're Jews, aren't they?" he said and took off up the steps.

The Executioner turned back to the work in progress. He counted each load the forklift stacked on the pier, mentally adding them to those already there. It wasn't that he didn't trust Isaac, and he damn sure didn't care if Advance-Tech got stiffed on the deal.

But the Executioner intended to know exactly how much ammunition they took on board.

And where every last bullet went.

When the last of the ammo cases had been piled on the pier, Isaac came down the ramp carrying a clipboard. The Israeli captain frowned as he walked toward Bolan, then glanced up toward the bars in the distance and nodded knowingly.

He handed Bolan the clipboard and a ball point pen. "I don't envy you your job," he said. "Not with a man like Van Doorn." He pointed to a line at the bottom of the yellow inventory receipt. "Sign here."

Bolan took the pen and wrote Al Giddings on the line.

A man wearing dirty blue dungarees and black, thick-lensed prescription sunglasses led the crew from the *Pegasus* down the ramp. The forklift began carrying the cargo up the brow. As it made each trip, the ship's boom swung over, took the freight and swung it across the deck before depositing it in the hold.

Bolan heard footsteps behind him and turned as Van Doorn came down the steps. The South African walked far too straight and stiff to be sober.

Van Doorn halted next to him and smiled at him moronically. "Everything go okay?" he asked, his voice slurring slightly.

"There wasn't a lot to it, Van Doorn."

The South African nodded and glanced back over his shoulder. "Great. You're doing a good job, Giddings." He brought his wrist close to his face, staring at his watch. "I'm almost finished," he said, jerking his head back toward the street. "Keep up the good work." He climbed the steps once more and turned back to the Purple Parrot.

It was midmorning by the time the ammo had been loaded onto the ship. The man wearing the sunglasses walked over to Bolan. "Jones is the name," he said. "I take it you're with Van Doorn?"

Bolan nodded.

"I'm the skipper." He pulled the sunglasses from his face and wiped the thick lenses with the tail of his T-shirt. "And I don't mind tellin' you I got no use for the Boer bastard. It's a damn loose ship we run," he spit as he squinted away from the sun. "And it's that drunken bastard's fault." Jones finished wiping his glasses. "You a seagoin' man?"

"On occasion."

"Yeah. What I figured. Well, we'll see if you're any better than that inebriated buffoon. He sober enough to board?"

Bolan shrugged. "We'll find out."

"Suppose we will." Jones shoved the glasses back on his forehead. He turned and led the rest of the crew on board.

The Executioner started up the steps to the street. A million rounds of 9 mm ammunition had just been taken on by the Advance-Tech ship. No matter what Webster had planned, it couldn't all be going for that mission. No, some of it would be sold along the way. To whom, he had no idea.

But he intended to find out.

Bolan pushed through the ragged screen into the Purple Parrot. Stopping just inside the door, he scanned the room. A pale, emaciated young man in his early twenties twirled toward him on a bar stool. The kid wore a blue shirt, unbuttoned and knotted above the waist. He'd been a little heavy with the purple eye shadow and lipstick. He smiled hopefully toward the door, saw Bolan, then turned back toward the bar.

A few other early-morning drinkers had already taken up residence in the Parrot. Among them was an old man they'd passed earlier on the dock. He sat alone at the end of the bar, a duck-head cane propped against his leg. He spit tobacco juice into the saw-dust-covered floor as the Executioner passed.

Bolan spotted Van Doorn at a table in the corner farthest from the door. The man was whispering into the ear of a woman with grimy, unkempt black hair. She cackled hysterically at whatever he'd said, her thin lips receding to reveal brown gums and several missing teeth.

Van Doorn looked up as Bolan approached. His eyes faltered for a moment before focusing on the Executioner. Then the South African's face lighted up like a Christmas tree. "Giddings!" he bellowed. "Sit down and have a drink!"

Bolan looked at the beer and shot glasses covering the table and shook his head. "The ship's loaded. We're ready to sail."

Van Doorn's eyebrows dropped as he struggled to understand.

"The *Pegasus*," Bolan said. "The shipment's on board. It's time to go."

The man's bottom lip dropped as the message sank in. "Oh, yeah," he grumbled. "Shit." He turned to the woman at the table. "Another time, darling," he said and rose to his feet.

The South African took a step around the table, caught his foot on a chair leg and went sprawling to his face on the floor. He giggled like an imbecile as Bolan hauled him back to his feet. "Giddings, you old bastard," he said. "Let's shove off!"

Disgust filled the Executioner as he guided Van Doorn out the door of the Purple Parrot.

"Giddings, you're all right." Van Doorn burped as they started down the street. "Even if you did fuck up my fun last night."

"The last thing we needed was cops around," Bolan said.

The South African halted and nodded. "Right you are, mate," he said, his bloodshot eyes staring up at Bolan. "You're right, you're right, you're right." He shook Bolan's hand from his arm and weaved toward the pier.

Van Doorn stopped just before the steps and turned back. "But as soon as this is over, what do you say we get some kaffir bitches and do them up right? Some that can't be traced by the pigs, eh?"

Bolan felt the revulsion course through his veins. He forced himself to smile. It took every ounce of self-discipline the Executioner had to form the words. "Sounds good, Van Doorn."

The man cackled again and started down the steps. Halfway to the bottom he tripped, rolled onto the dock and came to rest flat on his back, laughing hysterically.

Bolan descended the steps. He was bending over when he heard the voice behind him. "Need any help there, mate?"

The Executioner turned to see the old man with the glass eye leaning on his cane at the top of the steps.

He shook his head, gripped Van Doorn under the arms and jerked him up. The South African's laughter ended abruptly. Tears formed in the corners of his eyes. "I fell," he moaned. "Bloody fuckin' hell, I fell, ah, my knee...." He began sobbing in low growls. "The kaffirs, Giddings. The bloody kaffirs have caused all this."

Bolan nodded. "Sure, Van Doorn. It's not your fault. But you're drunk. And didn't Webster tell you to stay away from the booze?" The Executioner paused, letting it sink past the alcohol.

Slowly Van Doorn's face changed to a mask of fear.

"What'll he do if he finds out, Van Doorn? Fire you? Or kill you?"

The South African's face answered the question for him.

Bolan nodded. "Don't worry. I'll take over. You get into your cabin and sleep it off."

"No...hell. I'll be all right. I'll—"

Bolan turned him to face the ship. Jones was watching from the deck, the sun reflecting off the thick lenses covering his eyes. "You can't let the men see you like this," he said.

"Why not?"

"Do you trust them? All of them? Can you be sure none of them will tell Webster?" He paused, then went on. "I'll handle things until you sober up. But you'll have to tell me where we're headed, and who we're dealing with in case you're still out when we get there."

Van Doorn nodded. Slowly, his lips moving mechanically, he slurred, "Basques, mate. The fuckin' ETA. Don't have the foggiest what they've got in store, but they're takin' half the ammo off our hands in Lisbon."

Bolan took a deep breath. "How about the rest? Where's the other half go?"

Van Doorn's eyes closed and he started to fall again. Bolan held him up. "The rest of the ammunition, Van Doorn. Where's it going?"

The South African's eyes opened briefly, then his lids fell once more and he slumped against Bolan.

The Executioner carried the man to the ship and shoved him toward a man in a Kansas City Royals baseball cap. "Take him to his cabin," he ordered. "I'll take over from here."

The man in the cap nodded.

Bolan turned back toward the pier as the *Pegasus* cast off. He watched the churning water below the hull as Antwerp began to fade across the water.

And wished he could have just dropped Deetlev Van Doorn into the sea and been done with it.

THE ANGRY WAVES QUIETED as the *Pegasus* passed into the English Channel. Bolan stood at the rail of the main deck, watching the turquoise waters darken to a deep indigo. The harsh wind battering his face dropped to a gentle breeze. Above him, the hovering rain clouds that had followed them since Antwerp finally stopped, and the sun slipped out to cast its rays down onto the sparkling water.

The Executioner entered the superstructure and mounted the steps to the flying bridge, shifting his weight with each roll of the ship. He stuck his head into the bridge. "Where's Jones?" he asked.

The radioman looked up. "Gone below," he said in a slow, West Texas drawl. "Asleep, I imagine." He shook his head. "Man's got demons in his soul. Can't sleep for shit in the nighttime, but come daybreak tornado couldn't wake him."

"What's your name?"

"Lacy."

Bolan nodded. "Weather report?"

"Most likely clear all the way. Little rain and wind, maybe. Nothing big."

The warrior nodded and walked back out to the bridge. His gaze fell below to the strange deckhouse forward of the bridge. Rising twelve feet into the air, a series of switches decorated the port side of the housing. The top structure split down the middle and clamped together with rusted brown hinges.

Bolan had taken the first few minutes of the voyage to familiarize himself with the ship. He'd found a large quantity of C-4 plastique in the hold next to the ammo. He'd inspected further, checking the upper deck of the ship and the small cabins and twin holds below. Though the Executioner's wars had been fought more often on land than sea, he'd taken to the water enough times that he found little on most vessels that raised his eyebrows.

This mysterious metal deckhouse was an exception. The Executioner had no idea what it hid.

He watched the water continue to darken as the ocean floor fell farther beneath the freighter. He wondered briefly why Webster had trusted this assignment to a drunken incompetent like Van Doorn. A man didn't become as successful as the Advance-Tech CEO by distributing responsibilities carelessly. Particularly in his line of work.

But people changed, Bolan reminded himself. Sometimes, as they became successful, they lost sight of the traits that had made success possible. The visit to the château near Hasselt proved that creature comforts had taken a highly important place in Webster's life. Perhaps they were clouding his judgment.

The rest of the morning was uneventful, and it was late afternoon when Van Doorn mounted the ladder and joined Bolan on the flying bridge. The Executioner noted the dark, drooping circles under the South African's eyes. The skin on the rest of the man's face had faded to the hue of sour milk.

Van Doorn didn't speak at first. He grasped the rail and stared out across the sea as if he might throw up. Finally he turned to Bolan. "Don't think you've made any points, mate," he said. "Something's wrong with you. Real wrong." He stopped, coughed, then spit phlegm over the rail into the sea. "You passed up a free piece of ass last night, then you spoiled mine."

Bolan turned to him. "Van Doorn, you were about to kill her. If the cops had shown up—"

"Bullshit." His eyes narrowed, the lids dropping low to form slits of flabby flesh. "Webster could have taken care of that." He spit over the rail again. "And why'd you want to know where the ammo's going so god-awful bad?"

"Look, Van Doorn, I was trying to do you a favor. As drunk as you were, I couldn't be sure you'd even be awake when we got there."

From the bridge behind him, the Executioner heard a sudden pounding. He turned to see Lacy's fist hammering against the glass. Bolan turned and ducked into the bridge, followed by Van Doorn.

Radio static filled the room as Bolan entered. Lacy looked up from the console excitedly, pointing toward the radar screen mounted on the wall. "Three high-speed targets," he drawled, "approaching from all sides . . . and closing in faster'n a prairie fire."

Bolan leaned forward, studying the screen. "Establish radio contact," he ordered.

Van Doorn spoke behind him. "Wait a bloody minute, Giddings. *I'm* in charge, here." He tried to push past Bolan to the screen. The Executioner didn't budge.

Lacy keyed the mike. "*Pegasus* to approaching fleet, *Pegasus* to approaching fleet . . . identify." He killed the button, and static filled the bridge once more.

They waited. Nothing.

"Try again," Bolan ordered.

Lacy nodded. "*Pegasus* to approaching fleet . . ." After a long moment, the radioman looked up at Bolan. "Don't know who the hell they are," he said, pointing back to the screen, "but I can tell you this. They're quicker'n a two-dollar whore. Closing in at close to twelve knots."

Van Doorn threw open a drawer in the desk and jerked out a set of binoculars. He burst through the door onto the bridge. Bolan followed as the South African pressed the eyepieces against his forehead and rested his elbows on the rail.

"Bloody fucking hell," he breathed, smiling wickedly over the binoculars. "We're about to have some fun."

Bolan yanked the binoculars away and peered through the lenses. Skimming across the top of the water, directly toward the freighter, he saw the lines of a cigarette boat. Quickly he circled the bridge. He saw two more of the long, slender craft coming fast at forty-five-degree angles.

The warrior sprinted back to the South African's side as the man screamed down to the main deck. "MacKenzie!"

A moment later, the man in the Kansas City Royals cap mounted the ladder.

"Get your crew on the gun," the South African ordered.

MacKenzie cupped his hand over his eyes and stared across the sea. "Should I wake Captain Jones?"

Van Doorn shook his head. "Let the four-eyed son of a bitch sleep."

"How about the rest of the men?" MacKenzie asked.

"Negative." Van Doorn grinned. "We won't need them."

MacKenzie turned away. Bolan grabbed him by the arm and spun him back. "Get them ready, anyway, MacKenzie. You've got weapons aboard, I assume?"

"Well, pistols mainly."

"Wait a minute, Giddings," Van Doorn sputtered.

Bolan ignored him. "Arm the men, but keep them out of sight for now."

The man descended the ladder, then disappeared into the hole.

Van Doorn stared at Bolan. "I told you, I'm in charge, Giddings." He stomped back to the rail and gazed across the water at the oncoming speck.

MacKenzie and three other crewmen hit the deck below and sprinted toward the deckhouse near the bow of the ship.

Van Doorn continued to watch the three power-boats as they sped toward the freighter. His grin widened. "Pirates. Bloody fuckin' pirates." He turned to Bolan once more and shook his head. A cocky smirk rode his features. "But it's no problem, Giddings. I've got a little surprise for them."

Bolan saw the man in the Royals cap lean down and flip several switches on the deckhouse. The rusty hinges squeaked in protest as they opened. The housing split down the middle and the sides fell outward.

The Executioner sprinted down the ladder to the main deck. He helped the four men lift the metal sides and set them out of the way.

A thin layer of brownish-red rust covered the large gun that appeared. Bolan recognized the weapon as a 3-inch .50 caliber. Popular on U.S. destroyers in World War II, the gun was a hand-loader and required a crew of four to operate. The hundred-and-fifty-inch shells would devastate the cigarette boats. If the 3-inch functioned properly, it would be like hunting squirrels with the Desert Eagle.

The warrior studied the rust coating most of the gun and training stand.

The operative word was "if."

"Ready the weapon!" Van Doorn shouted from the bridge. The smile stayed on his lips as the pointer, trainer and loaders took their places around the gun. The trainer jumped into a metal tractor seat, glued his eyes to the sight and swung the barrel toward the nearest of the oncoming boats.

The pointer depressed the barrel as he peered through his own sights. Satisfied, he secured the gun in place as MacKenzie rammed a shell into the breach and slammed it closed. He pressed a button at the rear of the weapon, and a sharp crack assaulted the men's ears.

The giant three-inch round hit the water fifty yards to the left of the oncoming boat.

"Turn the bloody barrel!" Van Doorn ordered. He raced down the ladder and crossed the deck.

The trainer's hands flew on the wheel. A moment later, MacKenzie fired again. The round plunked into the water twenty yards to the right of the advancing craft.

Van Doorn bellowed like a gut-shot bull. He shoved the trainer to the deck and slid into the tractor seat. Furiously he began to revolve the wheel.

Bolan heard a high-pitched screech as the turret jammed and locked into place.

The South African leaned into the pedals, straining to move the wheel. "Bloody fuckin' hell!" he screamed, rising to his feet. Sweat poured down his face. "Just shoot the fuckin' thing!"

MacKenzie pressed the trigger. Again, the round flew high to the right.

The Executioner dropped to his knees, grasping the hand grips of the training stand. He leaned in, the muscles of his arms and shoulders threatening to burst as he strained to dislodge the jammed mechanism.

The turret didn't budge.

"Help him, dammit!" Van Doorn shouted to the other four men.

Bolan looked up. The lead cigarette boat was less than a hundred yards away. Too close now for the big gun. He heard the craft cut its engine. The boat began to drift toward the freighter.

Lacy's voice came over the loud speaker. "Captain, we've established radio contact."

"Patch it through out here," Bolan shouted.

Van Doorn shot daggers from his eyes. "I'm...in charge," he mumbled. His voice sounded less sure.

A moment later, the scratchy sounds of radio static came onto the deck. Then a voice with a heavy French accent said, "*Pegasus,* this is Captain Jean-Pierre Le Champ of the *Preying Mantis.* My instructions are simple. You will lay down your arms and surrender your cargo, or you will die."

The Executioner rose as the speedboat floated closer. He peered across the water. On the starboard side of the ship, he heard the other two speedboats cut their engines. He turned to MacKenzie. "Are the men armed?" he asked.

MacKenzie nodded. "Like I said—pistols, a couple of Uzis...."

"Any grenades?"

The man frowned. "Yeah. A few, I think. In the black locker, first hold." He stopped, then said sheepishly, "We'd counted on the 3-inch."

"Then you should have taken care of it," Bolan replied. "Get below. Tell the men to stay put for the time being. No sense in showing our hand until we have to."

Van Doorn grabbed him by the sleeve. "Goddammit, Giddings. I told you *I* give the orders around here!"

"Not anymore."

MacKenzie looked quickly at Van Doorn, then disappeared down the ladder. The pointer, trainer and the other loader took off after him.

As the speedboat floated closer, Bolan saw half a dozen men on deck. They wore a variety of flashy costumes. Sunlight bounced off the steel of the submachine guns and assault rifles in their hands.

Bolan crossed the deck and descended the ladder. In the first hold, he found the locker and stuffed two fragmentation grenades into the side pockets of his jacket. Two more went into the front pockets of his slacks.

Fifteen men stood nervously in the hold, handguns stuffed in their belts. The Executioner studied their frightened faces. They weren't soldiers. Sure, they might be capable of cutting someone's throat in a back alley of Shanghai, but they weren't accustomed to stand-up, head-on fighting.

Bolan turned to address them. "We're surrounded. Outgunned, maybe outmanned. The only thing we've got going for us is surprise." He paused, looking into the terrified faces. "They've got rifles, we've got pistols. That means we've got to let them get into range before we do anything." He turned and grasped the rail of the ladder. "Stay below until you hear my first shots. Then hit the deck and start shooting as if your life depended on it." The Executioner paused again. "Because it does."

He climbed back up the ladder and reached the main deck just as the *Preying Mantis* pulled alongside, the two ships' hulls banging together. The Executioner walked to the rail, his hands held open and high above his shoulders. He glanced down and saw that a six-foot freeboard differential separated the rails of the two vessels.

The *Pegasus* had high ground, always an advantage.

Maybe their only advantage.

The men on the deck of the speedboat trained their weapons upward, their fingers on the triggers. A familiar face stepped to the bow.

The old man looked up at the Executioner, a sneer on his face. He'd changed from the tattered clothing he'd worn on the docks in Antwerp. The duck-head cane was still gripped in one hand, but an Uzi pistol extended from the other. "Where's your crew?" he called up.

"Below," Bolan answered. "I assume you're Le Champ?"

The pirate captain smiled, bowed low at the waist and swept the cane dramatically across his body. "I am Le Champ. And what may I call you?"

"Death," Bolan replied.

In one smooth movement, the Executioner drew the Desert Eagle from inside his jacket and squeezed the trigger.

The smile had no time to leave the pirate's face as a giant .44 Magnum drilled through the man's right eye and out the back of his skull.

Bolan dropped beneath the rail as the pirates returned fire. Assault rifles and subguns sang out over the open sea, their deadly rounds flying over the Executioner's head before drilling through the superstructure.

Van Doorn hit the deck, pulling the Tanarmi 9 mm from under his shirt. "You're bloody nuts!" the South African screamed.

Bolan rolled to his knees, extended the Desert Eagle over the rail and double-tapped the trigger. One massive Magnum round downed a pirate in a frilly pink tuxedo shirt. The other .44 drilled through the chest of a bearded man holding an AK-47.

Return fire drove the Executioner back to the deck. Behind him, footsteps sounded from below as the crew of the *Pegasus* raced up the companionway. Past them, on the other side of the superstructure, Bolan heard the squeaking sounds of hull against hull as another of the cigarette boats came alongside.

MacKenzie and another man burst onto the deck. A Smith & Wesson Model 59 gripped in both hands, MacKenzie fired over the Executioner's head at the pirates. A volley of rounds from a subgun blew him back against the superstructure. He stumbled to the rail, leaning over, as another barrage of 9 mm's riddled his body. He fell to the deck.

The man behind MacKenzie wore a black watch cap. He stood in the middle of the deck, spraying a hundred-and-eighty-degree arc of 9 mm rounds toward the pirates with one of the ship's Uzis.

The Executioner took advantage of the diversion to down a pirate with a long, flowing handlebar mustache. Bolan squeezed the trigger, sending the first round through the man's neck. The pirate's throat erupted like a crimson fire hose as the bullet severed the jugular vein. An M-16 fell from his hands, bounced across the speedboat's deck and splashed into the sea.

The Uzi ran dry. As the crewman struggled to ram another magazine up the grips, a dozen rounds of enemy fire tore through him. He fell forward to the deck, the subgun still gripped in his hands.

Bolan saw another head rise quickly from the hold of the freighter. The crewman glanced around, then ducked back down.

The Executioner's jaw tightened. The crew had given up. He'd gotten all the help from that quarter he was going to get.

The warrior dropped back to his hands and knees, crawling along the rail, out of sight below the hull. He heard scratching noises, and then the hooked ends of a white PVC ladder curled over the rail in front of him.

A pirate wearing a blue silk shirt, his hair tied back in a ponytail, scampered up the ladder.

Bolan let him reach the rail, then tapped twice more on the Desert Eagle's trigger. The man fell back out of sight. The warrior moved to the PVC ladder, flipped it into the water, then continued around the super-structure on all fours. The freighter rocked beneath him as the third cigarette boat neared, sending its waves bouncing off the freighter's hull. The sound of plastic against plastic squeaked through the sudden silence as more of the ladders hooked the side of the *Pegasus*. Next came the dull thuds of feet hitting the deck as more the pirates leaped over the rail.

Bolan readied the near-empty Desert Eagle with a full mag, then shoved it back in his holster. Drawing the sound-suppressed Beretta 93-R from shoulder leather, he thumbed the selector switch to 3-round bursts as he rounded the side of the superstructure.

A pirate wearing a green bandanna had just climbed over the rail, facing away from the Executioner. The sling of an M-16 circled his neck.

Sudden gunfire rang out from behind the Executioner, who resisted the urge to turn.

But the noise caught the attention of the man in the green bandanna. He twisted at the waist, his eyes widening in surprise when he saw the Beretta staring him in the face.

Bolan squeezed the trigger once. A point-blank, 3-round burst of 115-grain 9 mm slugs slapped wetly between the pirate's eyes at 1150 feet per second. The man fell to the deck as the green bandanna darkened to black.

Bolan whirled as running footsteps replaced the gunfire. He raised the Beretta, holding it chest-high.

Lacy rounded the superstructure and stopped in his tracks, the ship's other Uzi dropping from his hands.

The Executioner swept the subgun from the deck and handed it back. He motioned silently for the radioman to stay put, cover that side of the ship. Lacy nodded and crept to his rear, pressing his back against the superstructure.

Bolan crab-walked to the pirate with the M-16 and pried the rifle from the man's fingers. He tugged hard on the sling, snapping the thin metal eye hook. Dropping the 20-round magazine, he checked it. Full. He then shoved the Beretta into its armpit holster and peered over the rail. The second cigarette boat rocked softly in the waves next to the freighter, its deck deserted.

That meant the rest of the crew was either hiding below, or already on board the freighter. They'd be moving around to the other side of the ship, hoping to come up on him from behind.

Bolan grasped the M-16 in one hand and pulled a grenade from his jacket. He jerked the pin, then heaved the deadly orb over the side and into the speedboat.

The grenade dropped past the ladder into the pirate's hold. A second later, the Executioner heard a dull explosion.

He moved cautiously around the superstructure, hearing the sounds of gunfire from the other side of the ship. Stifled moans drifted toward him as the clamor quieted. The Executioner rose, peering out over the sea.

The third boat had drifted a hundred yards away across the waves. Four men crouched on deck. They showed no signs of moving closer to enter the foray.

The Executioner continued around the deck, passing the jammed 3-inch gun. He'd almost come full circle now. If more pirates had boarded from the second boat, he'd confront them soon.

Or they'd come face-to-face with Lacy.

The sudden burst of automatic rifle fire blasted the Executioner's ears. He sprinted around the superstructure, glancing over the rail on the run.

The first boat still floated next to the freighter, the deck empty.

Suddenly the gunfire stopped. Bolan headed to Lacy's position. The radioman lay in a bloody pile on top of four pirates, two more of the invaders standing over him, their backs to the Executioner.

The two pirates entered the gates of hell never knowing what hit them. The Executioner squeezed the trigger of the M-16, firing off a precise figure eight that kicked both men into a macabre dance of death.

Suddenly the seas were again quiet. Across the water, Bolan heard the racing engine of the third cigarette boat. He turned toward the bow.

Footsteps rounded the superstructure from the other side. Bolan raised the M-16.

Van Doorn appeared, the Tanarmi held in front of him. His eyes widened, and he lowered the automatic when he saw the Executioner.

Bolan grabbed him by the shirt collar, raising him to his toes. "Anybody besides Lacy able to steer this thing?" he demanded.

Van Doorn's head bobbed up and down. "MacKenzie," he gasped.

"MacKenzie's dead," he said. "Who else?"

"J-Jones."

"Get him behind the helm. And get me a sound-powered phone to the bridge."

Van Doorn stared stupidly at him.

"Now!" Bolan dropped him.

The man turned and ran toward the bridge.

Bolan raced to the jammed 3-inch gun.

The third cigarette boat skimmed away across the waves as the Executioner slid into the trainer's seat. He tried once more to turn the stand, his arms straining against the bicyclelike pedals. The rusty iron groaned, squealed, then one of the grips snapped off in his hand.

Van Doorn returned with the phone. The Executioner slipped the headset over his ears. Positioning the microphone in front of his lips, he said, "Jones?"

"Aye." The voice still sounded half-asleep.

"Wake up and get ready. What's the lowest speed you can establish steerage?"

"About five knots."

"Then build speed to five. And keep it there."

"Aye, *sir,*" Jones said sarcastically. Bolan heard a chuckle over the headset. "And if you can pull this off, I'll—"

"Just do it and shut up," Bolan told him. He watched the speedboat as it continued to race away. Jones was right. It *was* a long shot. It would require concentration, split second timing...and luck.

The *Pegasus* began to coast through the water, moving at a ninety-degree angle from the escaping cigarette boat.

Bolan's eyes froze on the pointer sights. He lowered the three-inch gun, steadying the barrel on a spot just above the horizon as the freighter increased speed.

Jones called through the headphones. "Five knots."

"Come right," Bolan ordered.

The ship began to turn.

Bolan gripped the pointer with one hand, waiting as the barrel turned slowly into line with the fleeing pirate ship. "Slower!" he shouted into the microphone.

The vessel slowed, and the barrel inched maddeningly around. "Come right," the Executioner said again. "Come right . . . come right . . . come right . . ."

The pointer sights fell on the escaping pirate ship. "Hold!"

Bolan pressed down on the trigger button, and a giant 3-inch shell exploded from the gun. He watched through the sights, waiting, as the round flew over the waves toward the cigarette boat.

A dull plunk sounded across the water as the shell found its mark. A moment later tiny flames leaped from the deck of the pirate boat. Then the craft exploded, turning the blue horizon into a blazing red-and-yellow inferno.

4

The streets of Lisbon were a flurry of activity as the cabdriver headed downtown. Bolan noticed a curious mixture of East and West, as modern hotels and skyscrapers sprang up between ancient cathedrals, Renaissance monasteries and Moorish castles.

Entering the Alfama district, the cabbie steered through the winding, casbahlike streets. People representing every country, race and life-style crowded the bazaar. Once the hub of the Portuguese underworld, organized crime in Alfama had fallen to perhaps the only enemy powerful enough to chase it elsewhere—tourism.

The native kiosk operators still wore traditional Moorish robes. The carts and tiny booths hustled ceramics, hand-painted glass and gold filigree jewelry, giving the old quarter an Arabic flavor found few places west of Istanbul.

Next to Bolan in the back seat, Van Doorn sat sulking. The South African had hit the bottle again right after the pirate attack, drinking himself into oblivion. After a short period of rage in which he appeared ready to challenge the Executioner, he'd passed out and been carried back to his cabin. Van Doorn had slept through the remainder of the afternoon and night, coming alive again only minutes before the *Pegasus* sailed into Lisbon.

Bolan studied the man as the taxi continued past stands selling fresh lobster, tuna and salmon. Both of Van Doorn's hands were pressed against his temples. For the time being, the hangover made him docile. But the Executioner knew that when it wore off, there'd be more trouble. He'd made Van Doorn look bad in front of the Advance-Tech crew. The South African had not only proved he was incapable of leadership during times of crisis, he'd shown the yellow streak down his back by disappearing as soon as the shooting started.

Cowards were dangerous. The Executioner reminded himself not to turn his back on the man.

The driver turned a corner, and they passed a street band playing eerie, minor-key Arabic music, then slowed as they neared a café. The sign over the door read El Fatima. On the sidewalk outside, dark-skinned men in brightly colored caftans hawked Madeira linens, lace and cork-lined cigar humidors.

Bolan and Van Doorn exited the vehicle. The South African turned back to the driver. "Stay here, mate," he said. "We'll be right back."

The Executioner followed Van Doorn across the sidewalk, stopping him at the door. "Who are we meeting?" he asked.

Van Doorn rubbed his head again. "Some bloody Spaniard's all I know."

"How are we supposed to know him?"

"He'll find *us*. Just follow my lead." Van Doorn paused, then dropped his hands from his head. "Or," he said sarcastically, "you can just run the whole fuckin' show yourself if you want, you're so bloody smart."

Bolan shook his head. The man had sunken to childishness. "Van Doorn," he said, "let's go in, do the deal and get out of here. I don't like your company any better than you like mine. But we've got a job to do. Let's get it done."

Van Doorn squinted through his piggish eyes. Finally he nodded.

They stopped just inside the door, letting their eyes grow accustomed to the sudden darkness. Two dozen tables were scattered across the floor. Bright flames glowed on each of the tables, casting ghostly shadows around the room.

A maître d' wearing tails and white tie appeared from nowhere and stood before them. He frowned slightly, then said, "English?"

"Yeah, English," Van Doorn replied.

The man led them to a corner table, lighted the candle, handed them menus and turned away.

"Don't open it," Van Doorn said.

"Why?"

The South African shook his head. "Just set it on the table. Upside down and closed." He dropped his menu before him.

Bolan followed suit.

A moment later, a tall, swarthy man rose from a table across the room and approached them. "Advance-Tech?" he asked.

Van Doorn nodded.

"Sit down," Bolan said.

The man hooked a chair leg with his foot, pulled it back and slid into the seat. "English?" he asked.

"Yes, fuckin' bloody English," Van Doorn replied, his hands returning to his head. "Let's get this done and get the hell out of here. What's your name?"

The tall man paused, looking from Van Doorn to the Executioner. Though Bolan had allowed the South African to take the lead, the man across the table seemed unsure who was in charge. Finally he turned to face Bolan. "Our...goods are in port?" he asked.

Bolan nodded. "Ready when you are."

The man smiled. Ignoring Van Doorn, he extended his hand to Bolan. "You may call me Francesco," he said.

"Giddings," Bolan told him. He shook the hand. "You ready?"

"Yes."

Van Doorn spoke up hopefully. "Anybody want a drink first?"

Bolan just looked at him. He and Francesco rose to their feet.

The South African followed Bolan and Francesco out of the café to the cab. The Executioner took the front as the other two men slid in back.

They remained silent during the long, winding ride back. When they reached the docks, Van Doorn paid the driver and they walked along the quay toward the *Pegasus*.

The Executioner's trained eyes studied the docks as they neared the ship. They'd passed several groups of hard-looking men, speaking Spanish rather than Portuguese. That in itself was hardly peculiar considering the geography. But each time they had neared, the voices had fallen to whispers, and the men had studiously avoided eye contact.

Basque terrorists? Portuguese cops staking out the transaction about to take place? Some of both?

Bolan didn't know. But he'd find out soon enough.

The warrior followed Van Doorn and Francesco up the bow to the freighter. They descended the ladder to the hold, and Van Doorn pointed to the cases of ammo stacked along the wall. "Five hundred thousand rounds of it's yours, mate," he said. "Now, let's get it the hell off the ship so we can get out of here."

Francesco nodded. Bolan and Van Doorn followed him back topside.

A few minutes later, a dozen men boarded the *Pegasus*. Bolan recognized several from the walk along the docks. The ship's boom raised the ammo cases to the main deck, and the men began hand-carrying them toward a convoy of three canvas-covered flatbed trucks that had backed onto the pier.

The Executioner stood next to Van Doorn on the main deck, watching the transfer. The openness of it all was shocking. No attempt had even been made to disguise the shipment. "Parabellum" and "9 mm," as well as the Israeli Military Industries logo, screamed in bold lettering from the sides of each ammo case.

"Where are the cops while all this goes on?" Bolan asked Van Doorn.

The South African snorted in contempt. "Probably in the nearest whorehouse, spending the money Webster pays them."

Bolan and Van Doorn stood at the bow, watching as the Basques continued to unload the cargo. The Executioner knew he couldn't just let Francesco walk away with a load like that. Growing out of an anti-Franco student movement in the early fifties, the ETA was one of the oldest and better organized terrorist groups in the world. They'd carried out untold numbers of kidnappings, executions and bombings over the past two decades.

A half-million rounds of ammunition was enough to supply their clandestine, hit-and-run strikes for many months to come.

The Executioner racked his brain, trying to come up with a plan. If he sabotaged the shipment now, and Van Doorn or another of the Advance-Tech men noticed, his undercover work would come to a grinding halt.

But if he let Francesco and his men get away with the ammunition, many of those 9 mm rounds would find a final resting place in the bodies of innocents.

Bolan saw Van Doorn shifting his weight nervously from leg to leg again. The Executioner recognized the symptoms. He turned to the South African. "You trust these guys?"

Van Doorn looked at him like he'd grown an extra head. "I trust nobody, Giddings."

Bolan shrugged. "Fine. I was just thinking it's a waste of time watching the whole procedure. I could use a drink."

Van Doorn's eyes lighted up with new enthusiasm. "Giddings, you might turn out all right after all." He turned toward the bridge.

Behind his thick sunglasses, Jones stared down at them.

Van Doorn waved him down. "Jones," he said as soon as the man reached the main deck. "Watch these sons o'bitches and make sure they don't take more than their share. Giddings and me've got some important paperwork to do."

"Didn't know gin came in paper bottles," Bolan heard Jones mumble under his breath as he followed Van Doorn across the deck to the ladder.

DEETLEV VAN DOORN'S HAND trembled as he struggled to get the key in his cabin door. Even little things like this were getting to be a struggle. He didn't ask for much, Van Doorn thought as he poked at the lock. All he wanted was... simplicity. Yeah, simplicity. The older he got, the more he liked things simple. Easy. He liked drinking his "head kicks" of gin and beer. He liked sleeping them off. But most of all he liked screwing kaffir cows, then cutting their throats.

When he was in a position where he could get away with it, of course.

The South African continued to struggle with the key. Right now, nothing was simple. Nothing was going the way he liked it.

Van Doorn sensed Giddings moving up behind him. The big man took the key ring from his hand.

"They're tricky, sometimes," Giddings said. "Let me try." The big man slid the key into the lock and twisted.

The door swung open. Van Doorn shot through the opening like a sprinter coming off the blocks. He went immediately to the cabinet above the small stainless-steel sink, yanked open the door and pulled out two large water glasses. Digging further, he found an un-opened bottle of Geneva gin. "Ah, virgin," he muttered under his breath.

The full liter bottle brought a smile to his lips. Just a few seconds more. He'd feel better. Have his head on straight again, and these damned bloody shakes would go away.

He turned back to Bolan as he twisted the cap. The big man had taken a seat in the armchair across from his bunk.

Van Doorn poured a full glass of gin. He guzzled half of it and felt the fiery liquid burn past his throat and tickle his stomach. He shuddered, lifted the glass again and drained it.

The South African stared at the glass, then looked up as the shaking calmed. "Ah, Giddings," he said. "Where's me bloody manners?" He poured two fingers of gin into the other glass. Not too much. Don't give him too much. Don't want to run out.

Van Doorn handed Bolan the glass and watched him take a sip. Bloody fuckin' bastard. He hated men who drank slow. Almost as bad as men who didn't drink at all.

An old maxim of his ex-wife's father ran through his brain: *Never trust a man who doesn't drink.*

Right, mate. Right you were.

Moving to his bunk, Van Doorn took a seat. He held the glass in one hand, the bottle in the other as the gin began to course through his veins. He felt happy, safe, almost silly.

Across from him, Giddings took another sip, and the South African's mood suddenly changed. Fuck him. Little tiny fucking baby sips. Bloody bastard has no idea how to have fun. Always in control. Always doing the right thing at the right time.

Van Doorn smiled across the cabin as he filled his glass again.

Have fun, mate, Van Doorn thought. Your bloody days are numbered. I don't know how, quite yet. But I'll get you.

The South African thought he saw Giddings's eyebrows lower. Had he frowned? Why?

Sweat broke out on Van Doorn's forehead. He hadn't spoken, had he? Said the words out loud? He'd *thought* those things, not said them.

Hadn't he?

Van Doorn took another gulp of gin. He was drinking too much again. It affected his judgment. Christ, he didn't even know if he was talking or thinking.

Another swig. Giddings was still sitting there. Calmly. No, he hadn't said it out loud. Okay. Good. As soon as this shit was over, he'd cut down. No, hell, he'd just fuckin' quit drinking altogether.

From here, they'd sail south to Tangier. He knew he wouldn't be able to stay away from the French wine there, but as soon as that delivery was over...

The South African drained his glass and poured another. He felt his entire body began to glow, and his good spirits returned. He set the bottle on the table next to the bunk. Yeah, he'd quit drinking altogether. When Webster had talked to him—*threatened* him, he'd cut down. At least until this trip. He could do it again.

The South African tried to focus his mind on Webster. The image was fuzzy. Webster had threatened to kill him if he didn't stop drinking. Would he really do it? After what Van Doorn had done for him?

Maybe.

Van Doorn drank half his glass. He wouldn't have started on the booze again, if it wasn't for this bloody bastard sitting across from him. Fuckin' Giddings had driven him to it.

The familiar cobwebs started in his head. They seemed to come quicker than they used to when he drank. From somewhere far away, he heard a voice. "How about another?" He looked at the obscure image in the chair, and wondered for a moment who the man across from him was. Oh, yeah. Giddings.

Giddings's arm was outstretched, his glass empty.

Van Doorn reached for the bottle, knocking it over onto the table. He lunged after it as the precious liquid rushed from the neck. Fuck it! Fuck it fifty ways to Sunday! He had only a few bottles left in the cabinet....

Through blurry eyes he saw Bolan rise from his chair and upright the gin bottle. The big man moved to the sink and came back with a towel.

That's right, you bloody bastard. Do everything right. Neat and spiffy. Just like the army.

The army. Right. Recon. He never should have left. There had been all the kaffirs he wanted. Men to kill. Cows to play with, then kill. Van Doorn felt the stir in his groin as he remembered the way the women had wiggled under him and his knife.

Van Doorn watched the man across from him mop up the spilled gin. He wondered again who the man was. Yeah, Giddings, right. But who the hell was he really? Where had he come from? Webster and Ulrikson hadn't told him shit, as usual. They never told him anything anymore.

The South African opened his mouth to speak. The words came out garbled.

He tried again, slowly forming the words with his lips. "Who *are* you, Giddings?"

Bolan shrugged. "Just a guy who needed work." He dropped the towel and lifted the gin bottle, pouring lightly into his glass and filling Van Doorn's again.

Bolan sat back in the chair. "You look tired," he said.

Van Doorn didn't answer. Tired. Yeah. But damn, he felt good. He took another drink, emptying his glass. He reached slowly for the bottle, careful not to tip it over this time. Almost gone. Better get up and get another.

"It's been a rough couple of days," Bolan said, and again the South African would have sworn his voice came from somewhere far away.

"Tell you what, Van Doorn. You get some rest. I'll make sure we don't get rooked on the ammo. What do you say we stay in port tonight?" He paused. "Where do we go from here?"

Van Doorn felt the grin forming on his face again. He knew it must look stupid. He didn't care. Giddings didn't know where they were going from here. But *he* did. That meant *he* was still in charge.

"For me to know," Van Doorn mumbled, "and you to find out." He set his glass on the table and pulled his feet up on the bunk.

Bolan stood and moved past him to the sink, opening the cabinet and getting out another bottle.

Van Doorn watched through a haze as Bolan placed the fresh bottle on the table in front of him. The big man moved to the door. "I'll take care of everything," he said as he opened the door and left.

The South African filled his glass again and lay on his side. What was Giddings up to? Was he trying to get *his* job?

Somehow, even through the foggy mist of alcohol, he knew that wasn't the big man's purpose. He hated to admit it, but the bastard was capable of a hell of a lot more than just filling the shoes of Deetlev Van Doorn.

Maybe it was Webster he was after. Yeah, that made sense. The big bastard might be trying to take over the whole Advance-Tech operation.

Well, the bastard wouldn't get it done. Not if Deetlev Van Doorn had anything to say about it. He'd tell Webster his suspicions about Giddings the minute they got to Belize. That would fix him.

Van Doorn drained the gin. The glass fell from his hand and rolled off the bed to the deck. He heard a distant crash as it shattered. The warm feeling had left his stomach, and he felt nauseous. He wondered if he ought to have another drink then take a nap.

He sat up and reached for the new bottle. Cracking the seal, he turned it up and held it to his lips. The sickness in his belly vanished and was replaced with a sudden, consummate fatigue. He felt as if he'd just run a marathon, or fought ten rounds in the ring. But damn, like they said, it was a good tired.

The South African lay back on the bunk. He'd take care of Giddings, one way or another. If Webster didn't believe him, he'd kill the bastard.

Everybody had to sleep sometime.

Deetlev Van Doorn closed his eyes and the world went black. Comfortable. Simple. The way he liked it.

BOLAN CLIMBED THE LADDER to the main deck. He stood at the rail next to Jones, watching ETA men tote the heavy ammo cases down to the waiting trucks.

Jones peered over the tops of his thick sunglasses at the clipboard. Bolan watched him count the cases and make a check mark each time one of the Basque terrorists passed.

The Executioner tapped him on the shoulder. "We're staying in port tonight," he said. "I'll be going ashore on business. Confine the rest of the men to the ship."

Jones looked up from the clipboard, nodded, then went back to counting.

Bolan watched Francesco secure the canvas flap at the rear of the second truck. The flatbed pulled up and out of the way, and the loaders moved to the final vehicle.

It wouldn't be long now. In a few more minutes, the transfer would be complete and the three trucks would pull away from the docks for parts unknown. If he didn't find out where they were going fast, he wouldn't find out at all.

Half a million potential victims were depending on him.

A Portuguese uniformed cop strolled casually down the dock. He stopped abruptly when he saw what was transpiring at the trucks, did an about-face and hurried away.

Bolan shook his head. It was time to make a few speculations, play the odds. In all probability, Francesco and his force would be heading back for northern Spain. While the ETA had expanded activities to include the entire country, the northern Basque mountains were still their seat of power. And a score of this magnitude would more than likely go directly to headquarters. Van Doorn had already told him the port authorities had been paid off. Officials along the road had probably had their palms greased as well. That meant the terrorists could afford to take the most direct route.

But what route could that be? Depending on their final destination, there were still several highways they might take.

Bolan watched as a man in olive green work clothes placed the final case on the bed of the truck. The next few minutes were crucial. Once the Basques left the crowded streets of Lisbon, a convoy like this would be easy enough to follow. But if he lost them in the city before he'd determined their course, he could kiss goodbye any plans of destroying the ammo... or the killers who planned to use it.

And he had one other problem. No matter where the Basques headed, if he planned to follow them, he'd need wheels of his own.

The Executioner retraced his steps across the deck and descended the ladder once more. He passed Van Doorn's cabin and heard loud, drunken snores through the door. In the hold, he glanced quickly around for prying eyes, then opened the footlocker containing the frag grenades and stuffed his pockets once more.

Francesco was on the main deck when Bolan returned topside. The tall, lanky Spaniard walked forward and extended his hand. "*Por favor*. Tell Señor Webster that the other half of the payment will be made in the manner designated."

Bolan shook the hand and nodded. He didn't know what arrangements had been made for payment, and he didn't care.

That payment would never be made.

The Executioner dropped Francesco's hand. "I have other business ashore," he said. "Any chance of catching a lift into Lisbon with you?"

Francesco's forehead wrinkled slightly. "We are on a very rigid schedule, Señor Giddings," he said. "To which part of town are you going?"

"North," Bolan said. "Near the road to Loures."

Francesco hesitated, then glanced back to the trucks. Finally he said, "You have done us a favor, amigo. The least I can do is to return the courtesy."

Bolan followed him down the gangplank as several of the men who'd loaded the trucks now climbed into the cabs. The rest of the terrorists faded from view, blending in with the crowds along the quay.

Bolan took a seat next to Francesco in the lead truck. He studied the man's face as the convoy pulled away from the docks and started through town. The ETA leader took several side streets, then pulled onto Highway E-3 and cut north across the city.

Like Rome, Lisbon had been built centuries before on a series of seven hills. To the side of the major thoroughfare, Bolan saw Gothic-style churches, museums and an old Moorish fort that had been renovated into a hotel. They passed the Estufa Fria, where turquoise streams and grottos ran under the park's many bridges.

Just past a large terrarium, another major expressway bent toward them from the west, then paralleled E-3 as they neared the north edge of Lisbon proper. The Executioner scouted the highway, looking for high ground. Ahead, he saw a gas station atop a hill. Next to it was a modern shopping center.

Motioning Francesco into the lot, Bolan pointed to a phone booth set against the side of the service station. "Let me out here," he said. "I've got to make a call."

Francesco nodded, pulled the truck to a stop and extended his hand once more. "Until we meet again," he said. "If we ever do."

Bolan smiled at him. "Got a feeling we will," he said and got out.

Bolan walked casually to the phone booth. Folding the door inward, he reached into his pocket as if looking for a coin.

The ETA convoy pulled back onto Highway E-3.

As soon as they were out of sight, the Executioner sprinted from the booth toward the shopping center. He had no time to choose between the dozens of vehicles parked in the lot. Coming to a year-old Chevy Blazer at the lot's edge, he took a quick glance around, then jerked the Desert Eagle from his hip and drove it through the window in the driver's door.

The glass was still settling as the Executioner shoved a briefcase and French beret out of his way and slid behind the wheel. Slamming the butt of the big .44 into the steering column, he split the hard plastic and ripped the covering away from the wires. Bypassing the lock mechanism, he integrated the ignition wires and the Blazer coughed to life.

The Executioner pulled out of the parking lot onto a side street leading to Highway 1. He raced through two red lights, dodging cars, ignoring their horns and hoping no Portuguese police were in the area.

When he reached the access ramp, Bolan twisted the wheel, bore down on the accelerator and climbed onto the parallel expressway. He stared back west to Highway E-3.

The ETA trucks were nowhere to be seen.

He stomped on the gas pedal again, forcing it to the floor. More horns blared at his actions as he threaded the Blazer through the heavy evening traffic leaving the city.

Topping the last of the seven hills, Bolan scanned the highway to the west. A half mile ahead, three tiny dots moved slowly north up E-3.

The Executioner eased up on the accelerator and dropped the Blazer back down to the speed limit. Now that he'd established visual contact, there was no sense taking the chance of getting stopped for speeding.

He glanced toward the sun as they continued north. Another thirty minutes and it would be dark. They'd also reach the village of Vila Franco, where the two thoroughfares merged. From there it was a short jog to Carregado. At that point, the convoy would either continue north toward Coimbra, or branch east to Santerum.

In either event, traffic would lighten. Witnesses on the road would be few and far between.

The Executioner would strike then.

Bolan kept the Blazer a quarter of a mile behind the ETA convoy. There was little chance they'd notice him on the parallel highway, but when they reached the junction, he'd have to fall in behind the trucks. And to carry out the plan that was forming in his mind, he'd have to eventually pass all three.

Bolan glanced to the beret on the seat next to him. It wasn't much of a disguise, but if he waited until dark, it might be enough.

The sun finally faded as they neared Vila Franco. The three trucks on the parallel highway switched on their lights. Bolan followed suit as they entered the village limits. He let a Volkswagen pass him just before the two roads merged, his gaze glued to the taillights of the rear truck.

The Executioner kept the Volkswagen between him and his prey as they angled back to the west, toward Carregado. The trucks stayed with E-3 when they reached the junction. The small German car turned off toward the east.

Bolan dropped his speed and fell back a few hundred yards. The darkened silhouettes of windmills stood out against the sky as they passed croplands and olive and cork groves.

Two hours later, they began climbing the hills toward the ancient Roman city of Coimbra. The Executioner let two cars pass, using them as a visual shield as they crossed the city limits.

The trucks pulled into a small, one-pump station on the western edge of town. Bolan halted the Blazer in the shadows a block behind. He stared down at the luminous hands of his watch.

Time was becoming a factor now. He needed to get the job done and get back to the ship before Van Doorn woke up and discovered he was gone.

The Executioner fell in behind as the trucks pulled out. They passed an ancient university, then an amusement park where children played in miniature castles, churches and cottages. Off and on, dark clouds drifted across the dim crescent moon, casting the night into blackness. Under the periodic half-light, the trucks started down the mountain on a winding secondary road toward Penacova.

Bolan followed a hundred yards behind. Five minutes later, he glanced up into the rearview mirror. Other than the trucks, the Blazer was the only vehicle on the dark road.

Which meant Francesco and his men would notice him soon. It was now or never.

Bolan donned the French beret and bore down on the accelerator. He turned his head to the Blazer's broken window, hiding his face as he sped past the trucks.

The Executioner rounded two sharp curves at breakneck speed, hit the brakes and brought the Blazer to a screeching halt broadside across the road. Jumping from the vehicle, he raced for a small grove of olive trees at the edge of the highway.

The Desert Eagle leaped from his hip to his hand. Bolan rested both arms in the vee of two branches, sighting down the barrel to a spot just behind the Blazer.

Clouds drifted through the sky, covering the moon again. The luminous sights of the big .44 stared back at the Executioner like eager, feverish eyes.

A few seconds later, Francesco's truck rounded the curve. The Executioner heard the tires squeal as the Basque terrorist hit the brakes. The vehicle skidded to a halt two feet from the Blazer.

The shriek of rubber pierced the night once more as the second truck rounded the curve. Hitting the brake pedal a split second too late, the driver sent his vehicle into a sideways skid. The truck halted, the passenger's door enmeshed with Francesco's bumper.

Francesco leaped from the cab. Cursing thunderously in Spanish, he pointed toward the blown rear tire.

The driver of the second truck and another terrorist dropped to the road. They stepped between the two vehicles and into the beam of the headlights.

The Executioner's first round roared through the night like an atomic bomb. Francesco's head snapped back, his body jerking spasmodically, and fell to the ground.

The two other men turned toward the trees, dumbfounded.

Bolan stroked the trigger again. The driver of the second truck joined his leader on the pavement.

The third man fumbled under his shirt, the darkened form of a pistol appearing in his hand. Disoriented, he ran straight toward the Executioner.

Bolan let him reach the trees, then fired once more.

The man's chest erupted like a volcano of red-hot lava. The concussion from the big Magnum round drove him back across the pavement toward the trucks, his legs pumping furiously under him as they fought to maintain his balance.

The Executioner squeezed the trigger again, and the terrorist flew back against the grille of his truck. Blood rained to the ground like a sudden scarlet shower.

The big .44 barked twice more, punching holes in the bodies of the trucks. Moments later fluid trickled from the gas tanks. The pungent odor of gasoline rose to the Executioner's nostrils as the fuel formed pools under the vehicles.

The third truck rounded the curve. Bolan caught a quick glimpse of the driver's startled face as he slowed, assessed the situation, then turned the wheel and raced onto the shoulder past the disabled vehicles.

The Executioner sprinted back to the Blazer. Leaping behind the wheel, he cut a sharp 180-degree turn, floored the accelerator and pulled up behind the truck.

As the terrorist vehicle increased speed, the Executioner saw the dark silhouette of a man climb through the window and crawl to the top of the cab.

The dark form slithered from the roof of the cab to the top of the cargo area. The short, stubby shadow of an Ingram machine pistol extended toward the Blazer as the man leaned forward onto his belly.

The Executioner heard the weapon's distinctive 9 mm cracks as the first few rounds obliterated the Blazer's windshield. He cut the wheel hard, swerving to the left as the second volley followed. Digging the Beretta from under his arm, he extended the barrel through the demolished windshield.

Before he could return fire, another short burst of 9 mm parabellums drove the Executioner below the dash. Watching the road as best he could, he swerved back right.

Ahead, the chatter of gunfire suddenly ceased.

Bolan rose back over the dash to see the shadow atop the truck struggling to insert another magazine into the machine pistol.

The Executioner didn't hesitate. Dropping the Beretta's sights on the man, he lined up the three luminous dots.

The truck swerved to the right as Bolan squeezed the trigger, throwing the Beretta's 3-round burst high to the left. The slugs skimmed across the top of the truck, missing the terrorist by inches.

The man on the roof swung the Ingram back into play. The entire magazine burst from the barrel, flying through the Blazer to take out what was left of the rear and side windows.

Bolan thumbed the safety, switching the Beretta to semiauto. Squinting through the darkness, he raised the sights, then dropped them once more on the shadow on the top of the truck and fired a lone parabellum.

He didn't see where the round hit the terrorist, but the dark form dropped the machine pistol and fell from the truck, hitting the pavement ten feet in front of the oncoming Blazer.

The Executioner bounced in his seat as the Blazer's front wheels jolted over the body, then rolled on.

He pulled off the road onto the shoulder. Throwing two-hundred-plus pounds onto the accelerator, he drew next to the window of the speeding cargo truck.

The driver jerked a revolver from under his jacket. A moment later, fire burst from the barrel and a sharp crack echoed above the straining engines.

The Executioner dropped the Beretta to the seat beside him, reached into the side pocket of his jacket and pulled free a frag grenade. Raising both knees, he gripped the steering wheel between them as both vehicles continued to race toward the bridge.

The Executioner pulled the pin and stretched his arm through the window. Directly ahead, less than fifty yards now, he saw the shoulder of the road drop out of sight beyond the bridge.

The driver fired again as Bolan heaved the grenade through the truck window, then stomped on the brake.

The Blazer skidded to a halt ten feet from the edge of the dark abyss.

Bolan watched through the shattered windshield as the truck continued under the girders, onto the bridge.

The terrorist vehicle was halfway across when a muffled explosion thudded dully back to the Executioner. Glass and metal flew from both sides of the cab. The truck veered to the right, crashed through the guardrail and dropped out of sight into the darkness.

Bolan inched the Blazer to the edge of the drop-off and hit the high beams. Fifty feet below, he saw the driver crawl from the overturned cab and stagger to his feet.

A second later, the gas tank erupted and the night lighted up like the fires of hell. The shipment of parabellum rounds popped and crackled like firecrackers as the flames ate through the cases to ignite the primers.

A sudden blaze shot from the truck, engulfing the driver. He ran madly right and left, his piercing screams cutting through the roar of the continuing explosions.

Bolan grabbed the Beretta from the seat and stepped from the Blazer. A lone mercy shot bore through the shrieking mass of fiery flesh to end the man's torment.

The warrior slid back into the Blazer and reversed away from the bridge. Cutting a fast U-turn, he raced back down the highway.

A bright red Alfa-Romeo had stopped next to Francesco's truck by the time he returned. A young man wearing a pressed white sport shirt leaned out the window, peering curiously at the bodies on the pavement.

Bolan pulled to a halt next to the sports car. He raised the Desert Eagle above the window, aimed it at the man and smiled.

The Alfa-Romeo set a new speed-start record as it screeched down the highway.

Bolan backed fifty yards from the trucks and stopped. Beneath the two vehicles, he could see the ever-widening pools of gas as the tanks continued to empty. Pulling another grenade from his jacket, he drew the pin and gripped the clamp tightly in his hand.

Holding the frag grenade outside the Blazer, Bolan raced back down the highway. Ten yards from the trucks, he opened his hand. The grenade bounded across the pavement, coming to rest in the pool of gas as the Blazer sped by.

He was a hundred yards past the two vehicles when he heard the roar. Easing up on the accelerator, Bolan glanced briefly to the rearview mirror, then turned his eyes back to the road as the ammunition began to pop like popcorn.

5

The lights of the ancient city of Tangier glowed dimly through the dusk as the *Pegasus* sailed into harbor. To the east, the gray silhouette of the Pillars of Hercules faded into darkness as night fell over the Strait of Gibraltar.

Bolan turned his eyes toward the stern as the crew began pulling in the lines. He watched silently while they looped the heavy ropes back and forth across the deck to dry.

Footsteps pattered across the deck behind him, and he turned to see Van Doorn walking steadily toward him. The South African wore a clean shirt and slacks. His wet hair had been slicked back over his skull, and a three-day growth of beard was the only clue to the binge he'd been on since leaving Belgium.

Bolan nodded and turned back to the sea. Van Doorn moved to the rail next to him. The freighter slowed, drifting through the water. Crewmen began tying the lines to cleats as the ship bumped to a halt at the dock.

"Who we meeting this time?" Bolan asked.

"Don't know who...just where," Van Doorn growled. His whiskey voice went with the beard—another dead giveaway to his debauchery.

The Executioner turned away, staring out across the water as the men continued to secure the ship. This was the first time he'd seen Van Doorn since returning from the assault on the Basques. The South African had still been sleeping it off, his thunderous, erratic snores threatening the ship's thin walls when the Executioner had returned in the early hours of morning.

Bolan had caught a quick hour of sleep in his own cabin, then gone topside to talk to Jones. All the man with the thick glasses had known was that they were sailing south to Tangier at daybreak.

"Ready, Giddings?" Van Doorn asked.

The Executioner nodded.

Three men in highly personalized, charcoal-gray military uniforms appeared as they started down the gangplank. A short, bulky man stepped forward as Bolan and Van Doorn approached. He smiled broadly, his white teeth flashing against black skin. A Sam Browne belt hung cavalierly below his waist, supporting a six-inch, nickel-plated Colt Python and a massive stag-handled Bowie knife. Stars glistened in bold relief on his green beret and both shoulder boards, announcing his rank.

"I'm General Mavimba," the man said in perfect Oxford English. "These gentlemen are my men." He hooked a thumb over his shoulder at the other two soldiers. "One of you is Van Doorn. The other is Giddings."

The South African extended his hand. "Van Doorn."

The general's smile faded slightly as he recognized the South African accent. He shook Van Doorn's hand quickly, then turned to Bolan. "Mr. Webster has made all arrangements. You will have no problems."

Van Doorn pulled a sealed white envelope from his jacket pocket and handed it to the general.

Mavimba's eyes darted back and forth across the docks. He snatched the envelope from the South African's hands and slid it under his tunic. Then, stepping quickly back, he raised a hand to his forehead in salute. With a last glance of distaste toward Van Doorn, he turned on his heel and walked away.

Bolan and Van Doorn made their way through the dock area to a long line of taxis waiting on the street. "Great Sacco," the South African told the driver as they slid into the back seat.

The driver wore a multicolored caftan beneath a bright red fez. He looked at Van Doorn in the rearview mirror and hesitated.

He'd picked up on the accent, too.

Finally the cabbie sighed, shook his head and twisted the ignition key.

Bolan watched the passing scenery as the cab headed toward the center of the ancient port city. For a while, they passed modern stores selling boat parts and other sea-related businesses. Then the buildings became smaller, more dense, and the obligatory blocks of seamen's bars and houses of prostitution appeared. The streets narrowed, then Tangier's Great Sacco casbah sprang up like something out of a late-night Errol Flynn movie.

"We'll get out here," Van Doorn told the driver.

The man pulled immediately to the curb.

The South African handed several Moroccan bills over the seat, and he and Bolan got out of the vehicle.

The combined odors of roast mutton, wine and sweating bodies filled the Executioner's nostrils as his feet hit the ancient cobblestones. Van Doorn led the way down the crowded street of shouting, bickering people. The influence of three countries jumped at them from all sides as they passed open stalls selling French wines, Spanish meats and Berber rugs. Men, women and children in both Eastern and Western dress—and every combination in between—sat at erratically scattered tables. They ate and drank wine, or glasses of the hot mint tea common to northwest Africa.

The Executioner followed Van Doorn past booths piled high with embroideries and ceramic figurines. Hawkers stood beside the flimsy stalls, trying to entice buyers to purchase their wares.

A few minutes later, they came to a stand selling ornate canvas slippers, and copper and silver serving trays. A tall, robust man wearing the woven goat's-hair cloak of the Berber sat on a stool behind the counter. A long stringy mustache fell past his chin, waving lightly in the breeze. Looking up from the newspaper in his lap, his quick gray eyes moved suspiciously from Van Doorn to Bolan. "What you like buy today?" he said in broken English. "*Babouches* for wives, eh, maybe?" His head leaned toward the slippers.

"Let's cut the crap, Hamid," Van Doorn said. "You *are* Hamid, right?" He didn't wait for an answer. "Where's Sabah?"

The thin man's eyebrows lowered. When he spoke, the broken English was replaced with a British accent. "Sorry, chap. Afraid I don't know who you—"

Van Doorn cut him off. "I said cut the crap. You're Hamid, right?"

This time, Hamid spoke in perfect English with an African accent. "That is the name my father gave me."

Van Doorn nodded. "Webster sent me."

The gray eyes flickered in recognition, and Hamid's thin lips curled back to expose several gold teeth. "Ah, yes. Mr. Van Doorn." He dropped briefly beneath the counter. When he straightened, he held several perforated tickets in his fingers. "Sabah will meet you this evening at eight o'clock." He handed two of the tickets to the South African. "I assume you will want to take your associate?"

Van Doorn didn't answer. He stuffed the tickets into his shirt pocket, and they turned away.

Bolan watched the South African as they started back up the street. Van Doorn's eyes flew from one wine stand to the next. On the outside, the man had made quite an attempt to clean up his act. But each booth they neared seemed to present a new challenge.

Finally Van Doorn stopped, looked at his watch and turned to Bolan. "We've got a couple hours. What do you say we eat?" Without waiting for an answer, he hurried to the closest stall. Bolan followed.

Behind the counter of the open booth stood a reed-thin man in a turban. He swatted impotently at the flies feasting on roast legs of mutton that hung from the ceiling. Steam and a potpourri of odors rose from pots along the counter containing meat, couscous and *pastillas*.

The skinny proprietor served a man with a German accent, dipping into the meat pies with a clay ladle and placing a large portion on a paper plate.

Bolan watched Van Doorn as they waited. The South African was studying the wine bottles stacked at the rear of the booth. His face was a road map of conflict as he fought the urge to have a drink. Sweat broke out on Van Doorn's forehead as he nervously shifted his weight from foot to foot. As soon as the proprietor turned to him, he grabbed the man by the sleeve. "Give us two plates of couscous and lamb," he said impatiently, pointing to the pots. "And a bottle of wine."

"What kind of wine?" the man asked. He pointed to the large assortment of bottles. "I have—"

"I don't give a damn. Whatever's cheapest."

Van Doorn already had the corkscrew of a Swiss army knife in the bottle by the time they found an empty table. He held the neck to his lips, guzzling half the wine as Bolan set the couscous on the rotting wooden tabletop. The Executioner ate quickly, watching Van Doorn as the man finished the wine and returned for another bottle.

The only things eating the South African's couscous were the flies.

Van Doorn appeared to calm down as the alcohol began to course through his veins. His eyes glazed over, and he swatted the flies away and hungrily downed the couscous. Several pieces of oily meat fell from the corners of his mouth to his shirt, staining the material. He didn't seem to notice.

When he'd finished, Van Doorn rose from the table. He walked unsteadily back to the wine stall, bought another bottle for the road, then returned to the table. "Ready, Giddings?" he slurred.

Bolan stared at the slovenly man. He shook his head in disgust. If Webster didn't wield so much power within the circles they were traveling, Van Doorn would have had his cargo ripped off and been killed long ago.

The Executioner stood. "Let's get a cab," he said, turning and starting back down the street. The South African shuffled after him.

Bolan glanced over his shoulder and saw Van Doorn pull the Swiss army knife from his pocket and pry frantically at the bottle. The knife fell from his hand to the sidewalk. He cursed, then bent to retrieve it.

Bolan reminded himself not to let his guard down. Deetlev Van Doorn might be a hopeless, bumbling, incompetent drunk, but that didn't mean he wasn't dangerous.

CAREFULLY PLANTED OAKS, elms and palm trees lined the gardens of the Mendoubia. Flowers of every variety bloomed around their trunks. A row of ancient French cannons sat among the gardens, adding to the breathtaking view that included every color of the spectrum.

The cabdriver sang along with the eerie Arabic music from the radio as they passed the Sultan's Palace. As they neared the smaller market area known as Little Sacco, the beach appeared in the distance. Dark-skinned Moors wearing bright silks, brocade and beads, robed and bearded Berbers carrying wooden staffs and tourists dressed in the clothing of various countries hurried through the streets toward the pavilion.

The driver stopped the cab in front of the immense building and Bolan got out. He held the door as Van Doorn drained the last of his wine, dropped the bottle to the seat and stumbled onto the pavement.

The Executioner reached out, pulling the tickets from the South African's pocket. Pushing Van Doorn up the ramp toward the main entrance, he paused as a young Frenchman dressed in a Dallas Cowboys T-shirt, designer jeans and hot-pink-and-neon-aqua socks tore their passes in half and ushered them through the door.

The hallways inside were a bedlam of confusion as people rushed to find their seats. Bolan ran interference through the pandemonium, pushing past vendors selling everything from soft drinks and nachos to hashish and opium.

The warrior found their box seats next to the ring. He pushed through the swinging, knee-level door and slid into one of the four empty chairs.

Van Doorn slumped lethargically next to him and closed his eyes.

The first fight of the evening was just beginning. Two tiny men—flyweights, by American standards—circled each other inside the ropes. Dressed in satin boxing trunks, they wore the usual gloves on their hands, but their feet were bare.

One of the fighters was Oriental. The other, a sinewy black man, had a long braid of hair that fell down his back from an otherwise shaved skull.

Bolan recognized the sport as he watched the two dance across the canvas. Thai-boxing—one of the most brutal forms of unarmed combat in the world.

Suddenly the black man moved in. Fists, knees and elbows flew in a flurry of motion almost too fast to follow. When they parted once more, blood streamed from the nose of the Oriental.

The Executioner settled back in his seat as the bell rang, ending the first round. The Oriental fighter dropped wearily onto the stool in his corner as his seconds pressed towels against his face.

Bolan looked up as the door to the box opened. His eyes widened slightly when a veiled woman entered the compartment. She swept her floor-length cloak to the side and entered the box.

The woman stood hesitantly, looking down at the Executioner. In countries farther east, it would have been unheard-of for a woman effecting purdah—the traditional female Muslim's way of life—to appear alone at an event like this. But in the more Westernized atmosphere of Morocco, the veil covering her face was only somewhat out of place.

Bolan studied the veil, realizing its true purpose. It doubled as a mask, providing an effective disguise.

The woman took a seat next to the Executioner. "This is box number fourteen?"

The warrior nodded. "You must be Sabah."

"And you are Van Doorn?"

Bolan shook his head. "Giddings." He tapped the South African on the shoulder and the man opened his eyes.

"I am Sabah," the woman announced.

Little sprays of saliva flew from Van Doorn's mouth as he sputtered incoherently.

"He's not feeling well," Bolan said. "I'll handle things."

The black eyes above the cloth flickered, then hardened. Sabah turned away from the drunken South African, her brows lowering in disgust. "If it was anyone but Webster with whom we dealt, even this small change in plans would make me consider aborting the transaction." She paused, then added, "But Webster and our Mutarabesun benefactor have dealt many times in the past. I will trust you. Allah be praised."

Bolan forced his face to remain deadpan as he heard the words. Mutarabesun—Ever Ready. A group of a hundred and fifty hard-core Muslim zealots hired to seek out and destroy the enemies of Libya—either real, or imagined so—by the madman of the Mediterranean.

Which meant their "benefactor" could be none other than the same uniformed lunatic.

For a moment, the Executioner wondered why a group with such direct links to Libya—and the equipment the crazed colonel could furnish—would waste time dealing with someone like Webster. Then the question answered itself. Mutarabesun operated primarily on foreign soil. It would be safer to obtain arms near the point of each strike of terror rather than transport ammo and hardware through countries that might not share Libya's enthusiasm for random killing.

"Everything's ready then," Bolan said. "I talked to the officials at the dock right before we came. You'll be covered." The Executioner turned back to the ring as the fighters came out of their corners for Round Two. He watched Sabah out of the corner of his eye as the man with the long braid drove the Oriental back against the ropes. "We can unload whenever you like."

Sabah turned toward the fight. The Oriental ducked under a left hook and leaped into the air, driving a knee into the groin of the black man. A sickening crunch sounded throughout the pavilion as the black man's plastic protective cup shattered.

The long braid swung through the air as he fell to the canvas, shrieking in agony.

The Oriental stepped forward, stomping down on the head and ending the shrieks.

"Then we will start immediately," Sabah said, "for we plan to sail later tonight." She paused. "Our vessel is the *Al Qatah*. We are anchored just over the horizon. I will instruct them to dock next to..."

"The *Pegasus*," Bolan said.

Sabah nodded, rose from her seat and started to walk away.

Bolan reached out, grasping her arm. It was time to take a chance. A hell of a chance. But he hadn't let the Basques take off with the ammo, and he didn't intend to turn a quarter of a million 9 mm rounds over to Libyan terrorists, either.

"Go ahead and start loading," he said. "My men will help. I'll come on board to work out the rest of the details then."

The Executioner saw her eyebrows rise. "We have already made the payment to Mr. Webster's numbered account in the Cayman Islands," Sabah said. "There are no more details."

Bolan nodded. "Sure. But don't you think we need an accurate count from both sides? That way, nobody can say they got ripped off later down the line." He paused, then added, "Look, I trust my men and I'm sure you trust yours. But it's not impossible that somebody loading—on either side of the deal—could get sticky fingers and decide on a little sideline sales of his own. We might not catch it until later. Then, the accusations start flying, and a good working relationship ends."

Sabah nodded. "Yes. I see your point. I will meet you on board later tonight. We will do the final count together." She grasped the hem of her cloak, whisked through the door to the aisle and disappeared down the steps of the pavilion.

Bolan watched the referee and judges drag the braided black man unceremoniously from the ring, down the aisle.

Two more fighters entered the ring. One wore a traditional tae kwon do uniform and black belt. The other was dressed in French savate shorts.

The Executioner turned to Van Doorn. The South African stared bleary-eyed into space.

"Let's go," Bolan said as he stood.

Van Doorn grunted.

VAN DOORN FELT as if his head had been stuffed with cotton as he followed Giddings down the aisle and out through the front door of the pavilion. He stood silently, weaving on the sidewalk, as the big man hailed a cab. Then, like a robot, he moved mechanically into the back seat. He slapped himself on the face. Dammit, he'd gotten drunk again.

The South African rubbed his face, trying to get some feeling into the numb flesh under the skin. He took a deep breath as his head began to clear.

Next to him, he saw Giddings watching, a curious expression on his face.

Van Doorn turned to him. Giddings had left the ship the night before and not returned until the wee hours of morning. He knew that much from Jones. Why? Where had he gone? What had he done?

He settled back in his seat and faced the front of the cab. Unless he missed his guess, the big bastard was trying to get him snockered again so he could do the same tonight. Well, that wasn't going to happen. Not this time around.

He was sobering up again, and he'd drink lightly from here on in. Watch the bastard. See what he was up to.

Van Doorn leaned forward and tapped the driver on the shoulder. "Municipal Casino."

The driver hit the brake and turned.

Bolan leaned over. "Don't you think we should get back to the ship? Make sure the Libyans don't rip us off?"

The grin widened on Van Doorn's face. He knew he must look stupid. He didn't care. "Hell, no, Giddings," he said. "Let the bloody wogs handle it. They know better than to fuck with Webster." He reached out, trying to put his arm around Bolan in a comradely gesture. "We'll go have a little fun."

Bolan caught the South African's wrist and placed it back on the seat between them.

The cabbie pulled up in front of another large building. Built in the Moorish tradition, huge pillars adorned the front steps below spiral domes that gave it an almost mosquelike appearance.

The South African watched Bolan pay the driver. "How about a little blackjack?" he said as they entered the building. He got no answer.

Men in tuxedos stood around the various tables. Their eyes glued to the games, they groaned or clapped their hands with each roll of the dice and deal of the cards. Women wearing long formal gowns stood next to them, adorning the room the way diamonds adorned their wrists, fingers and ears.

Van Doorn staggered toward the blackjack table, bumping into a busty black woman in a white gown. The glass in the woman's hand bounced against her chest, and the South African felt a distant stirring in his groin as drops of fluid rolled down the rounded flesh jutting over the top of her low neckline.

He reached out, lightly gripped the woman's shoulder and grinned at her. "Shorry."

He frowned as the woman recoiled.

Van Doorn stumbled to the table, shoving a young man in a white dinner jacket out of the way. He took a seat and stared foggily at the dealer as Bolan dropped into the chair next to him.

The dealer dealt cards to both men. Van Doorn placed his ante on the green velvet tabletop and looked at his hole card. Seven. Bloody fuckin' seven of diamonds. With the eight he had showing, that made what...fourteen? No, dammit, fifteen. "Hit me," he murmured.

The dealer dropped the ten of spades in front of him.

"Fuckin' bloody thunder!" Van Doorn boomed throughout the room.

The noise in the casino suddenly quieted. The gamblers and their women stared across the room toward the source of the outburst.

Van Doorn felt his face redden as the dealer swept away his cards and money.

Next to him, Van Doorn heard Bolan say, "Blackjack." He turned in his seat in time to see the big man flip a face card over and drop it next to the ace he had showing.

Anger raced through the South African's veins. Couldn't this bastard do *anything* wrong? He tipped one of his glasses toward the ceiling and chugged it down.

Van Doorn picked up his cards. A thin whiff of perfume swept into his nostrils, and he was vaguely aware of someone approaching on the other side of Bolan.

"Good evening," a low, sultry voice murmured.

He turned toward the sound to see a tall, willowy brunette. The thick, bushy hairs over Van Doorn's eyes lowered. He struggled to focus on the milk-white breasts that strained against the sequined evening gown.

The most lovely woman in the world, Van Doorn thought. A goddess. Venus. "Good eve—" he started to say, then stopped.

She was talking to Giddings.

"My name is Madeline," the woman said to Bolan in French-accented English. "May I sit down?"

Van Doorn felt himself scowl.

The dealer dealt. Don't bust again, dammit, Van Doorn muttered under his breath. Ten. Ten of spades. And the eight of clubs. Eighteen. Right? Right. Stick. The South African stared up at the dealer and shook his head.

The dealer tossed a card to Bolan, then dropped the nine of clubs on top of his own hand before turning his hole card over to show the queen of hearts. Nineteen.

Van Doorn glanced to his side. Giddings, of course, had a ten, a six and a five. Twenty-one. Twenty-one again.

The South African pushed his cards toward the dealer and looked past Giddings to the woman. Madeline, she'd said. He felt the desire rise in his chest. Damn, he'd sell his soul—if he still had one— for a woman like that.

"That's one thousand American," Madeline said softly. "But it will buy a night neither one of us will ever forget. Anything you want." She paused. "At least, almost anything...."

Damn, Van Doorn thought, a bloody whore. He *could* have had her. If it wasn't for Giddings.

Bolan stood and turned toward him. "See you back at the ship in the morning," he said, and then he and Madeline were suddenly gone.

Van Doorn stared down at his hands. The anger he'd felt earlier suddenly returned tenfold. How come other guys got all the breaks? How come, just once, he didn't get a fair shake?

The South African inhaled his last drink and twirled in his chair. Some guys got all the luck.

Well, fuck the big bloody bastard. Sometimes, you made your own luck in this world. If you wanted something, you just went and took it. That's what he'd always done with kaffir cows.

Could Madeline be much different?

A half-formed thought took shape in the South African's fuzzy brain. Suddenly he knew how to get what he wanted...and take care of Giddings at the same time.

MADELINE LOOPED HER ARM through Bolan's as he ushered her down the steps of the casino to the nearest taxi. He held the door open, then slid in after her as the Frenchwoman purred a downtown Tangier address to the driver.

The driver turned halfway around in his seat, his eyebrows rising almost to his hairline.

Madeline cleared her throat politely and smiled back at him.

Bolan watched the driver as he turned reluctantly back to the wheel. He couldn't begrudge the man's unbridled awe. Madeline was beautiful.

The Executioner studied the long-legged brunette as they started down the street. When she'd first shown up at the table, he'd seen her as a quick answer to his problem. He could ditch Van Doorn, then her, and return to the docks to sabotage the Libyan ship. An easy job, considering the fact that the South African was drinking heavily again.

Bolan watched Madeline cross her legs and caught a quick glimpse of the black lace garter belt beneath the sequined gown.

Madeline smiled. Reaching across the cab, she took the Executioner's hand and squeezed.

Bolan returned the gesture. At least the part about ditching Van Doorn had been easy.

The driver steered the cab through the nightlife section of Tangier, watching the Frenchwoman intently in the rearview mirror. They emerged onto a well-lighted street of modern high-rise apartments, finally stopping in front of a shorter, four-story Gothic building.

Bolan got out and held the door for the woman. He paid the driver, then ushered her toward a giant black man in a braided doorman's uniform.

The giant grinned widely at Madeline. "Ah, good evening, Mademoiselle Rouillan," he said as he opened the door.

"Thank you, Kitwana."

The Executioner followed the woman down the thickly carpeted hall to the elevator and pushed the button. The doors opened and they stepped inside.

Once inside the privacy of her suite, Madeline announced, "I will freshen up. Please make yourself at home." She disappeared through a side door.

Bolan sat on a loveseat in the center of the room and studied the elaborate decor.

The apartment was reminiscent of Morocco's French colonial era. Tapestries and lithographs covered the walls. Framed in gold wood, Toulouse-Lautrec's women of the Moulin Rouge danced the cancan. Above the fireplace hung a large original painting by someone who had captured the Pont des Arts on the Seine River at night.

Madeline appeared suddenly, and the Executioner gave her his full attention.

The woman had discarded the sequined evening dress and now stood framed in the doorway. She wore black lace panties, seamed stockings and the garter belt he'd seen earlier. Her pale breasts jiggled provocatively above the half bra as she crossed the room toward him.

Getting rid of her would be an *easy* job, the Executioner reminded himself.

Madeline lowered herself alluringly to the love seat next to him and kissed him lightly on the lips.

Gently Bolan pushed her to arm's length, forcing his gaze from the half bra to her face. "We have something to talk about," he said.

Madeline snuggled closer to him, her lips pursing into a feigned pout. "What?"

"Price," the Exectioner said. "I want to double the thousand we agreed on."

Her surprise turned to mild concern. Then concern became skepticism, then fear. Madeline shrank back as if a spider had suddenly dropped between them. She glanced quickly toward the phone, then the door. "What is it . . . that you want?" she asked. "I do not do some of the things other women are willing to—"

"I'm not asking you to."

Madeline relaxed and looked at him curiously. "Then, what is it that you *do* want?"

"Nothing."

"What?" Madeline sat back against the corner of the love seat, folding her arms protectively across her breasts. "Do you find me unattractive? Or is there something wrong with *you?*"

Bolan laughed. "No, Madeline, I don't find you unattractive. And right now that attraction is reminding me that there's nothing wrong with me, either. But I need your help in another way tonight. I've got work to do."

"Then I will ask you again. What is it you would like from me for two thousand dollars?"

"Your word that if anyone ever asks, you'll say I spent the night with you here."

A false understanding registered on Madeline's face. Slowly she nodded. "You are some kind of criminal?"

"Some people think so." He rose from the love seat, reached into his pocket and peeled four five-hundred-dollar bills from the roll. He'd started for the door when he heard the sigh behind him.

Turning back, he saw Madeline cross her legs again. She ran her tongue slowly across her bottom lip. "Life is so strange in my profession," she purred. "I was thinking in the cab—you are a man I would be willing to sleep with free." She shook her head. "Take the back staircase at the end of the hall. No one will see you leave."

Bolan nodded and opened the door. As he descended the dark steps at the rear of the building, a grin tugged the corners of his lips. He pushed through the door into the alley.

An easy job? Well, some jobs were easier than others.

The Executioner gave Madeline one last thought, then forced his mind to the task at hand.

6

Two Libyans in OD fatigues guarded the *Al Qatah* from the edge of the weather deck. To the casual observer, neither appeared armed.

But as the Executioner came up the gangplank, his trained eyes picked out the bulge of the automatic pistols under their fatigue blouses.

As Bolan approached, the shorter of the two men held up his hand.

"You are Van Doorn or Giddings?" he growled.

"Giddings," Bolan said. "Sabah's expecting me."

The man's right hand inched closer to the weapon at his belt line. "We will see."

The other man turned to his partner. Without waiting for the order, he did a quick about-face and disappeared into the darkness across the deck.

The two men stood silently until the taller man returned. "Sabah is coming," he announced.

A few seconds later, the female terrorist stepped out of the darkness. All pretense of purdah had been left in her quarters, and she now dressed in the same fatigues worn by the men. The veil was gone, and beneath the penetrating eyes, the Executioner now saw yet another reason Sabah had covered her face.

The Mutarabesun woman looked as if she'd been shot at close range with a hot load of bird shot. Tiny black specks peppered her face and neck.

Bolan looked closer. No, she'd been in an explosion. A powder bomb of some type had gone off in her face. Considering the rough games played by the Libyans, she was lucky to have escaped with a face at all.

Sabah's hand went nervously to her face as she spoke. "You have not brought Van Doorn?" she asked.

"No."

"Good. My people are devout Muslims. We do not tolerate alcohol."

A curious philosophy, Bolan thought. Bombs, kindnappings and murders—fine. But no drunks need apply.

"Tell Webster we will deal with him no more if Van Doorn is involved," Sabah continued.

"I'll pass it on."

"I had expected you earlier," she said. "We are preparing to sail. Please hurry."

Bolan stepped on deck past the men. "You've already counted?"

Sabah nodded. "I am satisfied."

The Executioner's mind raced as the woman led him across the deck. There was nothing he could do to sabotage the ammo with Sabah watching. He'd have to come up with a plan to reboard the ship later. But how?

He glanced over his shoulder. The men guarding the gangplank showed no signs of leaving.

It wouldn't be that way.

As they descended the ladder to the hold, Bolan's eyes flickered toward the stern. Like the crew had done on the *Pegasus,* a heavy hauser had been left to dry on the deck. The thick line looped back and forth near a canvas-covered capstan.

Bolan ducked below deck level. If he could just get the line over the side without being seen...

The Executioner's eyes darted right and left, recording a mental blueprint of the ship as they passed the berthing area, the galley and then the engine spaces just aft of amidship.

The ammo was stacked against the wall in a small hold past the engine spaces. Scattered about the room were various engine parts, tools and other supplies.

Including a small spool of copper wire.

"You may count," Sabah said. "I will wait."

Bolan started at the far side of the hold, tapping each case lightly as he pretended to count. His mind continued to race. He had to distract Sabah long enough to get the spool of wire.

The Executioner worked his way through the cases, tapped the final box, then lifted the top case from the stack, set it on the floor and knelt next to it.

"What are you doing?" she asked impatiently.

Bolan didn't answer. He reached behind him to a stack of tools and found a large screwdriver. Jamming it under the lid, he pried up and began counting the boxes within the case.

Sabah stepped forward. "What are you doing?" she repeated anxiously.

"Look," he said, "if any of the men—yours or mine—got sticky fingers, they could've opened the cases, taken the ammo and replaced it with rocks, for all we know. I'm just making sure.'' He pulled the next case from the stack.

Sabah squatted next to him. "We do not have time to check them all."

"Just a spot check," Bolan assured her. He opened another case.

The Libyan woman jerked to her feet, exasperated.

The Executioner scattered more ammo boxes across the deck. "Two, four, six . . ." he said slowly.

Sabah dropped to her haunches once more. Her voice rose an octave. "I am *satisfied*. Now please leave." Eyes to the floor, she began shoving the boxes hurriedly back into the case.

Bolan kept one eye on the woman as he reached behind him and pocketed the small spool of wire. "Okay," he said. "But if you come up short, don't say I didn't—"

"We will not come up short!"

Sabah was still replacing the ammo when the Executioner left the hold. As he passed the berthing area, he saw several of the terrorist crew undressing by their bunks.

Good. That meant the Mutarabesun would have only a light watch out.

Bolan mounted the ladder to the deck. Glancing quickly around, he saw the two men still at the gangplank. Crouching in the darkness, he moved silently toward the stern to where the hauser lay. Dropping to one knee, he wrapped the end of the copper wire around the line, twisted several times, then tossed the spool overboard.

A faint splash rose from the darkness below.

The Executioner grabbed the hauser and wrapped the heavy line around a cleat near the rail. Securing it tightly, he rose to his feet and moved swiftly toward the hold.

Bolan was almost to the ladder when Sabah stepped back on deck. Her face contorted in skepticism as she saw him coming from the stern. "What are you doing?"

The warrior shrugged. "I'm a land man, myself. Just got my bearings off for a minute."

He walked past the guards and off the ship.

THE WATCH on board the *Pegasus* was as light as that of the Libyan vessel when Bolan returned to the ship.

Jones crossed the deck as the Executioner walked toward the ladder.

"Any sign of Van Doorn?" the Executioner asked.

The captain shook his head. "Somewhere inside a bottle, no doubt." He mounted the ladder to the bridge.

Bolan went below. He'd have to move quickly, now. The *Al Qatah* was already making preparations to sail. He had to get the explosives rigged fast.

If he didn't, a quarter of a million rounds of 9 mm ammunition would fuel the fires of the lunatic Libyan colonel.

Inside his cabin, Bolan dropped the Beretta and Desert Eagle into his bag. What he had to do next called for stealth, deception and role camouflage rather than firepower.

He'd have to go unarmed.

Moving to the hold, the Executioner broke open the crate of C-4 plastique. Cutting through the crate's plastic liner with his penknife, he reached in and sliced a slab of the claylike explosive from the lump.

Bolan moved on to a case of detonators against the wall. He pulled the first one from the box, carefully replaced the lid, then hurried toward the galley.

Digging through the drawers, he found a box of plastic freezer bags. He dropped the lump of plastique into one sack, the detonator into another and stuffed them both into his pockets.

The Executioner paused. He had everything he needed, except a timer.

He jimmied the lock on Van Doorn's cabin door and Bolan did a quick three-sixty with his eyes. A large wall clock hung above the berth; a clock radio was bolted to the table next to it. Both were too big to sneak on board or conceal once he rigged the bomb.

The Executioner searched quickly through the small closet, the drawers of the bureau, then the locker at the foot of the berth, coming up empty each time. He had to find something—an alarm clock, maybe. *Anything* that kept time.

And he had to do it fast. Time was running out.

Bolan glanced at his wristwatch and found his answer. He had another watch back in his bag. It was his only choice.

Moving swiftly back to the clock radio, the Executioner used his blade to remove the back cover. Reaching in, he ripped out several wires, jammed them into the plastic freezer bag with the detonator and hurried topside.

The quayside was almost deserted in the late-night darkness. Turning in the opposite direction from the *Al Qatah,* the Executioner walked past a British freighter, then two Spanish ferryboats. Taking a final look around for prying eyes, he secured the plastic bags in his waistband and dropped quietly into the water.

When he reached the Libyan vessel, he stretched one hand above the water, letting his fingertips brush lightly against the hull as he side-stroked around the ship.

Near the stern on the port side, the copper wire snagged his wrist.

The Executioner pulled slowly on the wire until the end of the hauser appeared against the starlit sky overhead. A sharp yank brought the thick line falling down the hull.

He grasped the rope and pulled until he felt it tighten against the cleat. Hand over hand, he began to ascend.

Bolan searched for movement as he grasped the rail and pulled himself on board. Other than the two men at the gangplank, the deck was deserted.

Crouching, ever ready for sudden surprise, Bolan drifted through the shadows toward the ladder. As he neared the capstan, footsteps echoed across the deck. He looked up to see one of the guards walking toward him.

The Executioner ducked behind the canvas-covered capstan as the man passed.

When the sound of footsteps had disappeared around the side of the superstructure, he hurried the rest of the way to the ladder. With a final glance, he dropped into the hold.

Loud snores came from the berthing area as the Executioner slipped silently down the hall. He paused at the door to the galley, peering around the corner.

Facing the wall, near the rear of the room, stood a sleepy-eyed terrorist. The man stared stupidly into the refrigerator, the door gripped open in his hands.

Bolan dropped to the deck and crawled past the opening, then rose to his feet and hurried to the engine room.

Swiftly he pulled out the freezer bags and removed the contents. Flattening the C-4, he molded it to the keel and inserted a detonator. He stripped off his wristwatch and pried off the back casing.

Eight a.m. should do it.

The Executioner connected the watch to the detonator with the wires he'd taken from Van Doorn's clock radio. He stepped back.

The bomb was planted firmly on the keel. From there, it should take out the boilers, blow a sizable hole in the ship and set off the diesel fuel at the same time.

By 0800, the *Al Qatah* would be safely out to sea, far away from the innocents on the docks and in nearby ships. The only ones to feel the Executioner's cleansing fire would be the Libyan terrorists.

The warrior crept back down the passageway and onto the deck. A moment later he was over the side.

BACK IN HIS CABIN, the Executioner stripped, dug through his bag for dry clothes and slipped his backup watch onto his wrist. He heard the horn of the Libyan ship sound as he slid the Beretta and Desert Eagle back into their holsters.

When Van Doorn didn't answer the knock on his door, Bolan twisted the knob and looked in. The South African's berth was empty, the covers still smooth.

The man hadn't returned.

It was almost 0400 when the Executioner mounted the steps to the deck. There were several possibilities as to where Van Doorn might be. The casino stayed open all night, and if the drunk was still on his feet, he might still be there. Tangier offered a multitude of other bars, as well, and the man might have taken up residency in any of them.

Bolan crossed the main deck and started up the ladder to the bridge, an uneasy feeling creeping through his soul.

There was another possibility.

Van Doorn might have consumed enough alcohol that he'd gotten mean and gone looking for a woman to rape and kill.

Jones was eating a sandwich when the Executioner pushed open the door.

"You seen Van Doorn?" Bolan asked.

The captain shrugged. "Thought he was with you," he said around a big bite of corned beef. He swallowed, then continued. "We're set to shove off at 0730. Want me to hold up?"

Bolan shook his head. "I'll find him."

The Executioner descended the ladder, crossed the deck and walked down the gangplank. Wherever the South African was, he had to find him and get him aboard. Each minute they delayed brought Webster's scheme—whatever it was—closer to reality.

A black cabbie wearing Western clothes and a cowboy hat got the Executioner quickly through the light traffic to the casino.

"Wait for me," Bolan said as he exited the vehicle.

Inside, the crowd had thinned. Only a half-dozen diehard gamblers sat wearily at the gaming tables. Van Doorn wasn't among them.

The same dealer stood at the blackjack table, tossing cards to an elderly man in a tux. "The guy I was with earlier," Bolan said. "You know where he went?"

The dealer looked up as he shuffled the cards. "The drunk?"

"Yeah."

"He got up shortly after you left. Went around hitting on the women until one of the bouncers had to throw him out." The man paused to drop a card in front of the player. "Thought there was going to be a fight for a while, but Big Ali can be pretty persuasive." He pointed to a black man in the corner who stood almost as wide as he did tall.

Bolan nodded. "Thanks." He turned and started away.

"One other thing."

The warrior turned back.

"He was asking everyone about Madeline. Where she lived. Things like that."

Bolan felt a chill run up his spine. "Did anyone tell him?"

The dealer pointed across the room. "You might ask Sylvie. She and Madeline are friends."

The Executioner crossed the room to where the short-skirted cocktail waitress who had served them earlier still moved between the tables, setting drinks in front of the players.

She smiled wearily at the Executioner as he approached. "I am so sorry."

"What?" Bolan asked.

"About your loss. Your friend—when he was trying to find you—he told me about the sudden death in your family."

"Did you tell him where Madeline lives?"

"Why, of course. He said it was urgent that he locate—"

Bolan turned and sprinted through the surprised gamers and out the door. Jumping into the back of the cab, he gave the driver Madeline's address. "Get me there quick," he said, holding a fifty-dollar bill in the air.

The man in the cowboy hat snatched the bill from his hand and pulled onto the street. Navigating the darkened streets with practiced hands, he ignored the stop signs and lights, and pulled up in front of Madeline's building.

The tall doorman was nowhere to be seen as Bolan sprinted toward the door. He twisted the knob. Locked.

He raced down the street, circled the block and raced down the alley to the rear door. He went to work on the lock with a small multipurpose tool he carried for such occasions.

The tumblers rolled, finally giving way to the makeshift picks, and the Executioner slipped inside.

Four floors above, he could hear Van Doorn's booming, drunken voice. "Open the fuckin' door, you bloody whore!"

Bolan took the stairs three at a time. When he reached the fourth floor, he saw the South African in front of Madeline's apartment, his face pressed against the peephole. The plastered Boer held a half-empty bottle of gin in one hand. With the other, he pounded madly on the door with the hilt of his survival knife.

"Open up, goddammit!" he slurred. "I got money!"

Bolan yanked the Desert Eagle from his hip holster and moved silently down the hall.

As Van Doorn brought a foot back, wavering unsteadily as he prepared to kick in the door, the Executioner brought the big .44 down on the base of his skull.

The South African grunted and slid to the floor, unconscious. The gin bottle and survival knife clattered across the hall.

The apartment door inched open to the end of the chain lock as Bolan knelt beside the unconscious man. His eyes fell on the big knife, which dripped blood.

Madeline peeked between the door and frame, then removed the chain.

Bolan looked up. "Are you all right?"

The woman nodded. She'd covered herself with a flowing, floor-length silk robe. "Is he dead?"

The warrior pressed his fingertips against Van Doorn's carotid artery. The pulse was fast, but steady. "No."

"Too bad," Madeline said.

Bolan gripped Van Doorn under the arms, hauled him to his feet and threw him over a shoulder. Without speaking, he walked down the hall to the elevator.

As the doors opened on the first floor, he saw why the big doorman hadn't been at his post—his body lay half-hidden behind a large planter on the other side of the hall.

Blood still seeped from the gaping slash in his throat.

THE TAXI PULLED UP at the docks. Bolan opened the door and got out as Van Doorn staggered to the concrete from the other side. The slovenly South African had regained consciousness during the cab ride, looked over at Bolan and asked simply, "What in bloody hell happened?"

Bolan hadn't seen fit to answer. He'd had all of the man that he could stomach. If he didn't still need to gain Webster's confidence for more important pursuits, he'd have rid the world of the homicidal maniac long ago.

As the Executioner mounted the freighter's gangplank once more, he gazed across the water and saw another reason Van Doorn would have to be put on the back burner temporarily. A dilemma of far more immediate priority stared him in the face.

In the shipyard across the docks, a giant overhead boom had pulled the stern of a ship half out of the water. Workmen on floats drifted around the propeller shaft, their hands busy with wrenches and screwdrivers around a large exposed screw.

Prominent gold letters on the side of the hull announced the ship's name: *Al Qatah.*

The Executioner glanced automatically at his wrist. The watch read almost 0700, and served as yet another reminder of what would happen in one hour.

Bolan and Van Doorn reached the deck of the *Pegasus.* The South African staggered toward the ladder leading down to his cabin.

Jones stood next to the rail, watching the repairmen at work on the Libyan ship. Bolan joined him, resting his hands on the rail.

"Came back about thirty minutes ago," Jones said without being asked. "Sprang a leak at the seal. Right where the prop shaft goes through the hull." He paused and snorted through his nose. "Stupid bastards."

Bolan nodded. "Take long to fix something like that?"

"Most of the day, I'd imagine." Jones turned toward Bolan. "But what the hell do we care, right? We're done with them. We'll be out of here in another thirty minutes." He turned back to the *Al Qatah.* "You found Van Doorn, I see."

The Executioner remained silent. He stared across the water to the Libyan ship. There were eight workmen on the floats next to the prop shaft. Several more stood on the dock, handing down tools.

A few early-morning tourists already strolled the quayside. By eight o'clock, the docks would be jammed with people of every nationality—chatting, laughing and taking photographs of the centuries-old international seaport.

Their laughter would end abruptly when the bomb exploded. The Executioner had set enough C-4 on the ship's keel to make this end of Tangier look like Hiroshima.

Bolan crossed the deck, descended the ladder and made his way directly to the mechanic's hold. Ripping open a cabinet, he found several toolboxes. Selecting a large crescent-shaped wrench, he slipped it under his shirt.

A gray-haired crewman met him in the passageway, nodded and moved on. Bolan waited until he was out of sight, then slipped into the engine spaces.

Bolan studied the engines. He needed something that wouldn't be readily spotted and fixed. Something hard to get to. Dropping onto his back, he slid along the deck to the wall.

In the corner of the cramped space, a small bolt clamped the fuel line to the massive engine. Bolan adjusted the wrench, wrapped it around the bolt and twisted.

A small hiss escaped the line, followed by the odor of diesel. Then a thin spray of fuel began to sprinkle from the line.

The Executioner slid back as the leak began to swell. Rising to his feet, he hurried back topside.

The lines had already been singled up when Bolan reached the main deck. Jones stood on the bridge. He held a walkie-talkie in his hand as he stared into the water alongside the ship, checking for obstructions.

"Let go forward," he said into the radio, then turned back to inspect their rear.

The Executioner mounted the ladder and stood next to him.

Jones turned to the bridge. "Right standard rudder... ahead one-third."

From inside the bridge came an excited voice. "Mr. Jones, engineering has a problem."

Jones's head jerked up. "What kind of problem?"

"I don't know. A fuel leak or something."

"Goddammit!" He ducked his head and sprinted toward the bridge. "Belay my last."

Bolan followed him into the bridge. Through the window, he watched the Al Qatah in the shipyard. Several of the terrorists loitered on and around the ship. A number of workmen now stood on deck just over where the others floated under the propeller.

With so many watchful eyes, there was no way he'd be able to slip over the side again without being spotted.

The Executioner felt a hard grin cross his face. He studied the workmen. They were dressed in a variety of work clothes and appeared to be of several nationalities.

Good. He ought to fit right in.

Jones ripped the phone from the man at the console. "What the hell is wrong?" he screamed, pressing the receiver against his ear. "What do you mean a leak! Yes... yes... I'm on my way." He slammed the phone back down and keyed the walkie-talkie. "Pass across forward line again," he ordered.

A voice on the other end said, "Come again?"

"Stop the damn boat!" Jones screamed.

Bolan followed the man down the ladder. The odor of diesel rose to meet them as they reached the main deck. Descending to the engine room, they waded ankle-deep through fuel.

Two crewmen stood sheepishly looking at the engines.

"What the hell's going on?" Jones demanded.

One of the men, wearing a diesel-soaked T-shirt, looked up. "We don't know, sir. It just happened."

Jones leaped forward, grabbed the man by the throat and slammed him against the wall. The thick sunglasses were an inch from the sailor's nose when the captain spoke. "That's what my first wife told me when I caught her with the preacher," he screamed into the man's frightened face. "Do I need to tell you what I did to *her?*"

The man in the cap shook his head and gasped out a raspy "No."

Jones dropped him. "Find it and fix it."

Bolan stepped forward. "How long is this going to take?"

Jones shook his head. "Depends on where the leak is, and how bad it is," Jones said. "If it's just a loose connection, it won't take long. If the line has to be replaced—longer. But what's going to take some time is the goddamn mess." He kicked at the diesel around his feet. "Got to be swabbed, washed down, then swabbed again."

Bolan nodded. "Notify me when you're ready to sail."

The Executioner strode down the passageway. With a quick glance over his shoulder, he ducked into the supply hold and pulled a soiled set of khakis from a hamper next to the washing machine. A bent and frazzled fishing cap and a canvas laundry bag lay among the chaos of the room. He stuffed the pants and cap into the bag and moved swiftly back to the mechanic's hold.

A small toolbox sat in the corner. The Executioner covered it with the canvas bag, then paused. Besides Sabah and the two men standing watch the night before, none of the Mutarabesun terrorists had gotten a good look at him. If he didn't encounter any of those three, he should be able to bluff his way through.

Bolan glanced in the mirror over the sink. There was no time to concoct a disguise that would pass scrutiny. If he met up with Sabah or the two men face-to-face, it would be over. But he needed something that would change his appearance enough to get by if they saw him from a distance.

Bolan hurried to Jones's cabin. Checking the passageway, he pulled his multipurpose tool from his pocket, slipped the tumblers in the lock and closed the door behind him.

The Executioner scanned the small room and stopped at an object on the counter next to the sink. He slipped the eyeglass case into his pocket and hurried to the main deck.

The crew paid Bolan no attention as he strode down to the dock. Climbing the steps to the street, he ducked into an alley. A moment later, he emerged dressed in the khakis and fishing cap with a pair of Jones's thick eyeglasses hiding his face.

Bolan dropped the spectacles low on the bridge of his nose, peering over the lenses as he walked. He crouched slightly, limping on his left leg to add to the role camouflage as he mounted the gangplank to the *Al Qatah*.

A short, tattooed Libyan with a full beard took a look at the toolbox and waved him on.

Bolan crossed the deck and started down the ladder. He was four steps down when he heard the familiar voice above him—the shorter guard he'd talked to earlier. He'd spoken in Arabic. Bolan didn't understand everything, but he knew trouble when he was up against it.

The Executioner kept his head down, shrugging.

"Parlez-vous français?" the guard asked.

"Oui," Bolan replied. He shoved the eyeglasses back up his nose. Letting the bill of the cap shield the top of his face, he raised his head and squinted through the thick lenses at the man.

"Where do you think you are going?" the man said in French.

"Below," Bolan answered. "Someone must check the connections to the engine."

"That has already been done." Bolan saw the man's eyebrows lower as he stared down, a curious look on his face.

"Look," Bolan said. "I only know I was told to go check again. If you don't want it done, I couldn't care less." He began to ascend the ladder. "You can explain it to the woman, not me."

The man held up a hand. "Who gave you your orders?"

"I don't know her name. The woman with the..." The Executioner tapped the fingers of one hand across his face.

Sweat broke out on the guard's face. He looked up and down the deck, his face flushed with indecision. "Go ahead," he finally said and turned away.

Bolan descended the ladder and walked down the passageway. He heard both laughter and Arabic curses as he passed the berthing area, and looked in to see several of the terrorists playing cards.

Bolan entered the engine spaces and slid the eyeglasses into his shirt pocket. He worked quickly, disconnecting his wristwatch from the wiring and removing the plastique from the keel.

The Executioner breathed a sigh of relief. He turned toward the passageway, then stopped. If he did nothing more, the Libyans would escape with the load of 9 mm rounds. How many of those rounds would be used to further their nefarious pursuits?

Bolan moved swiftly into the hold where the ammunition had been stored. The lid on one of the cases he'd checked the night before was still loose, and he set it ajar. He cut a small amount of the plastic explosive from the lump and dropped it into the case.

Just enough to get things started. Then the slugs would go off like a string of firecrackers on the Fourth of July.

Bolan reconnected his watch and set the time for 1100 hours. The *Pegasus*'s fuel leak should be fixed and the deck swabbed by then. They'd be on their way, and he'd watch the explosion from across the water.

Shoving the glasses back over his ears, the Executioner mounted the ladder, crossed the deck and left the ship.

JONES WAS STILL at the rail of the flying bridge when Bolan returned to the *Pegasus*. The Executioner raised a hand to the captain, crossed the deck and went below.

The source of the fuel leak had been located. A man wearing a ragged red sweatshirt lay on his back, tightening the fitting with a pipe wrench. Several other crew members swabbed halfheartedly at the pool of diesel, grumbling under their breaths as if it were the most exhausting task imaginable.

Bolan returned the captain's glasses to his cabin, locked the door behind him and went to his own tiny cubicle.

At 1050 hours, the warrior heard the engines fire up and mounted the ladder to the deck. He stood against the rail, watching the *Al Qatah*.

The workmen had finished at the prop, and the crew were making preparations to sail.

Jones gave one more order through his walkie-talkie and the *Pegasus* left port. The Advance-Tech freighter was two hundred yards from the docks when the bomb exploded.

The men on the main deck of the *Pegasus* turned in unison. The inverted, U-shaped boom supporting the Libyan ship's stern twisted and fell into the water, forcing the stern backward. The bow tipped up on end.

As if blown from the mouth of hell, red and yellow flames leaped from the hollow made by the split. A moment later, 9 mm parabellum rounds began crackling in the distance as if fired from a thousand submachine guns.

The workmen on the floats dived into the water and swam for the safety of the shipyard dock. On deck, two of the terrorists fell, slugs ripping randomly through their bodies. The others cowered behind capstans, deck housings and whatever other cover they could find.

Jones joined the Executioner at the rail. The bespectacled captain stared across the water as flames engulfed the terrorists' ship. "And we thought we had problems," he muttered.

7

A thousand feet below the big DC-10, the white-capped waves of the Caribbean rolled softly onto the beach. Bolan watched through the window, shifting slightly in his seat, as the plane dipped a wing and followed the coastline. Far in the distance he saw the dim skyline of Belize City.

The *Pegasus* had been at sea less than an hour when Bolan and Van Doorn had received the radio transmission to return to Tangier—Webster's order.

A telegram had been waiting. They were to transport the remaining half-million rounds of ammo and the rest of their deadly cargo to a small private landing strip halfway between Tangier and Ceuta, where an Advance-Tech plane would meet them.

The shipment was to be flown, rather than shipped, to Webster's jungle compound in Belize.

It didn't take Bolan long to figure out why.

The big operation, whatever it was, was being moved up.

Bolan, Van Doorn and the rest of the crew had spent the afternoon and evening on the road, transporting their freight by truck to the landing strip at the northernmost tip of Morocco. The Advance-Tech DC-10, converted from passenger to cargo use, had already landed. Under the watchful eye of bribed Moroccan officials, the plane had been loaded and had taken off for Central America.

The warrior turned back to the front as the DC-10 pilot spoke rapidly into the radio, alerting the tower near Belize City that they were about to begin their descent. The Executioner took special note that the man behind the controls didn't ask for permission. He *told* the controller they would descend.

As seemed to be the case wherever they went, Gus Webster had the local officials in his back pocket.

Several minutes later they passed over a long airstrip, chopped from the virgin jungle. The landing gear locked into place, and the converted cargo plane began its final descent.

Van Doorn stirred to life. "We there?"

The pilot nodded.

The plane touched down and slowed along the runway, turning to taxi toward a hangar that housed several smaller aircraft bearing the Advance-Tech logo.

Bolan and Van Doorn deplaned, watching in silence as a number of dark-skinned Indians unloaded the cargo and placed it in the beds of several half-ton trucks.

An elderly Indian with long gray hair tied back in a ponytail ground a rattling army jeep to a halt. Bolan and Van Doorn took seats in the vehicle. Without a word, the driver pulled away from the airstrip and followed the convoy of trucks along a narrow path cut into the thick trees.

Twice during the drive they had to halt, and word drifted back from vehicle to vehicle that the Indians ahead were clearing the road of fallen trees.

A lot of trouble, operating out here, Bolan thought. Remote. Far from help.

But far from prying eyes, as well.

An hour later, the convoy slowed to a crawl. Bolan saw a ten-foot fence topped with razor wire in the distance. Armed guards—Browning Hi-Powers with wooden stocks and 100-round snail magazines—checked each truck as they passed through the gate.

Van Doorn held up his hand as their turn arrived. A tall, rangy Indian waved them on.

Just past the gate, the trucks took a fork in the road and disappeared around a curve into the trees. The elderly Indian jogged the jeep to the left, onto a gravel drive, stopping in front of a sprawling one-story ranch house.

Bolan and Van Doorn exited the jeep and climbed the steps to the front porch. As Van Doorn reached toward the brass knocker on the door, the roar of another vehicle caused them to turn.

A blue-and-white four-wheel-drive Suburban turned off the road into the drive. The powerful, spotted body of a jaguar had been strapped across the hood of the vehicle. The big cat dripped crimson from a dozen bullet holes, its massive head bouncing up and down as the vehicle slid to a halt in a cloud of dust and gravel.

Gus Webster got out on the passenger's side, looking as if he'd just stepped out of the pages of L. L. Bean. A leopard band adorned his safari hat, and his pock-scarred face was half-hidden by the ever-present sunglasses. Webster had tied a bright silk scarf around his neck, and his khaki, desert-cloth bush suit was immaculately pressed, the pants bloused carefully into knee-high boots that still shined like they'd never left the store.

Ulrikson killed the engine and stepped out. He'd tied a black bandanna over his eyebrows to serve as a sweatband. The Viking battle-ax and massive .357 Maximum were both strapped to his waist.

A short powerful man in his late thirties joined the Swede. Near-luminous red hair covered the man's head, and he gripped an Uzi.

Ulrikson reached back into the Suburban and pulled two custom-made Champlin Firearms Classic rifles from a rack in the rear.

Webster grinned almost as widely as Ulrikson as the three men walked to the front of the vehicle. The Advance-Tech CEO paused to stroke the fur on the jaguar's neck. "Van Doorn! Giddings! Come here!" he shouted. He continued to pet the dead animal as the two men walked forward. "You ever seen a cat this big?"

Van Doorn moved next to the still-bleeding animal and looked up subserviently. "No sir," he said. "Where'd you bag it?"

"Not me." Webster chuckled. He tapped the rifle. "I only slowed him down. The rest is the work of our newest employee." He pointed to the red-haired man who stood with the Uzi. "Gentlemen, meet Mr. Sean Patrick Duggan."

Webster didn't wait for handshakes. "But the great part," he continued, laughing, "is there's more of them. Less than two klicks from here, they're thicker than flies." He turned to the gray-haired Indian who had remained in the jeep. "Get this cat into town, Coba," he ordered. "Tell Alonzo I want it fully mounted." He turned toward the house, then did an about-face. "And make sure to tell him I want a *snarl* on the lips this time. That last cat looked like something out of a Disney cartoon when it came back." Laughing again, he turned to Duggan. "Sean, go check on the trucks, then join us in the den." Motioning to Bolan and Van Doorn to follow, he mounted the steps to the porch.

After the heat of the jungle, the air-conditioned ranch house felt like the North Pole. The Executioner followed Webster through an enormous formal living room as Ulrikson disappeared with the rifles down a side hall. They came to another hall and passed a glass-enclosed office area, then entered a den that made the spacious living room look like a closet.

For a brief moment, the Executioner wondered if he'd just stepped into a zoo. Exotic animals of all species stared back at him from the floors and walls. Stuffed lions, tigers and leopards, their hind legs flexed in mock preparation to spring, posed on stands next to the couches and chairs. The heads of water buffalo, wildebeests and six enormous African elephant had been mounted on the walls, their glass eyes shining sightlessly. Arranged here and there among the more ferocious animals were a half dozen of the small-hoofed deer native to the forests of Belize.

Webster moved through the trophies to a smooth mahogany bar at the side of the room. "How about a drink?" he said. He pulled a six-pack of beer from the refrigerator and located an icy bottle of gin in the freezer above it. Turning back, he hesitated. "You *have* been behaving yourself, haven't you, Deetlev?"

"Of course, sir," Van Doorn said quickly.

Webster glanced toward Bolan for confirmation.

The Executioner stood deadpan.

Ulrikson's huge frame filled the doorway as he entered the room. He moved automatically to the bar and relieved Webster of drink duties. The Advance-Tech CEO dropped into a thickly padded armchair. "Sit down, gentlemen," he said.

Bolan and Van Doorn took seats across from him on the couch.

"I assume everything went smoothly?" Webster took a beer and shot glass from Ulrikson.

Van Doorn nodded. His eyes flew across the room toward the bottles on top of the bar. "No problems."

Ulrikson brought the two men their drinks, then took a seat in another of the armchairs next to a wildebeest. Van Doorn took a cautious sip of the gin, following it with a large gulp of beer.

Webster stuck his tongue into his shot glass, then set it on the coffee table next to the beer bottle in front of him. He stared at Van Doorn, his eyebrows lowering under the sunglasses. "So how did Mr. Giddings work out?" he asked as if Bolan weren't in the room.

Van Doorn downed the rest of his gin before answering. He turned away from Bolan, staring straight ahead to the Advance-Tech CEO. "I got my doubts about him, sir."

Webster raised an eyebrow and glanced at Bolan, then back to the South African. "Please explain."

"Well," Van Doorn started, stopping long enough for another chug of beer, "here's what happened. Take the first night we're in Antwerp, Mr. Webster. I find these two women for us. Nothing wrong with that, right?"

"Of course not," Webster said. "Everyone needs a little recreation . . . as long as it doesn't interfere with business."

"Well, Giddings here doesn't really seem interested. Or maybe he strikes out and gets pissed. For whatever reason, I'm laying the other bitch, and he bursts into the room and raises hell. The next thing I know, the cops are on their way and I've got to get him out of there."

Bolan stared at the South African.

"Then," Van Doorn went on, "in Lisbon, he disappears. Who the hell knows where he went?" The South African turned to the Executioner. "Didn't think I knew that, did you?" Looking back to Webster, he said, "And he shows up the next morning again like nothin' happened. Same thing in Tangier. He's gone—who knows where. And the fuckin'— sorry for the language, sir—the wog ship blows up."

"Yes," Webster said, his eyes flickering toward the Executioner, "so I heard. And what you may not be aware of, Deetlev, is that our Basque friends met with a similar untimely end."

Van Doorn's head bobbed up and down like an excited schoolboy impressing his teacher. He turned to Bolan again, a wide grin breaking out across his face. "That's what I mean, Mr. Webster," he said. "Every time he disappears, something weird like that happens." The South African took a deep breath. "And I'll tell you one more thing, sir. Giddings drinks like a bloody fish. When he wasn't doing a disappearing act, he was drunk—asleep in his cabin. No use at all." He paused, drained the rest of his beer and glanced nervously toward the bar.

Bolan didn't try to suppress the laugh that escaped his lips. Van Doorn might be incompetent as a leader, but he was a skilled liar. He used the tried and true, age-old tactic of sticking to the facts—just twisting the story to suit them a little.

"Well, well, Mr. Giddings," Webster said, and Bolan could see he was amused himself. "That's quite an indictment. Have you anything to say in your defense?"

Bolan stared across the room at the man behind the aviator glasses. It went against his grain to sit there defending himself, *auditioning* for a job with a man no better than the terrorists to whom he dealt arms. But if he expected to learn what master plan Webster had in store, he still had to rise past his present probationary status. And that meant playing the game.

The Executioner's teeth clamped tightly together. He forced a chuckle from his throat. "Oh, I've got a little to say. Primarily that if you'll take what Van Doorn just told you and swap his name for mine, you'll have a pretty accurate report of the drinking that went on while we were gone. Take a look at who's already finished his gin and beer and keeps looking toward the bar as if the bottle might sprout legs and run away."

Webster nodded. "But what of the unexcused absences, Mr. Giddings?"

Bolan felt his jaw tighten again. Unexcused absences? Webster sounded like a high-school principal talking to a student who'd cut class. "Guilty," Bolan said. He forced a smile. "But I'm human, too. I like women."

Webster leaned forward slightly. "What about the woman Deetlev had arranged—"

"I can't really get too excited about the disease-ridden females Van Doorn here seems to thrive on."

Webster turned back to Van Doorn. "Deetlev?"

"He's lying, Mr. Webster."

The CEO sighed. He stared at the South African, but spoke to Bolan. "This leaves me in a bit of a quandary, Mr. Giddings. I've known Deetlev for many years. And for that reason, I'm inclined to believe you concerning who spent the trip drunk in his cabin. Deetlev has his limitations, certainly, but he's been valuable to my operation. You, on the other hand, have shown superior skill. But Deetlev and Hugo both question your loyalty." He crossed his legs, carefully smoothing the wrinkles in his safari slacks. "I'm sorry, but at this stage of the game, I can't afford to take chances." He looked up at Ulrikson. "Hugo, if you would..."

The big Swede rose. The wild smile grew on his face as his hand fell to the grip of his pistol.

The Desert Eagle leaped into the Executioner's hand, the cocking hammer sounding like a cannon as it echoed throughout the room. Bolan leveled the .44 on Ulrikson's chest. The big Swede's hand froze on his weapon.

"Gentlemen, please." Webster shook his head in disgust. "Hugo, pay Mr. Giddings the amount we agreed upon. Then have Coba drive him into Belmopan when he delivers the jaguar."

"But, Gus—" Ulrikson began.

Webster waved a hand in front of his face, cutting him off. "Mr. Giddings knows nothing that can hurt us."

Ulrikson's grin faded slightly. His gaze glued to Bolan, he crossed the room, then disappeared down the hall.

Bolan reholstered the Desert Eagle, but kept his hand close to the grip. From down the hall, he heard the front door open. A moment later, Duggan appeared in the doorway.

"Ah, come in, Sean," Webster said. "Fix yourself a drink and have a seat. You're seeing one of the more unpleasant aspects of my responsibilities, I'm afraid. I've been forced to let Mr. Giddings here go."

Duggan swaggered across the room, lifted a bottle of Irish whiskey from under the bar and reached for a highball glass on the shelf against the wall.

Bolan turned back to Webster. He had to talk fast, convince the Advance-Tech CEO to keep him. Otherwise, he was about to find himself on the streets, no closer to Webster's operation than he'd been in Belgium. "Mr. Webster," he said, "here's the truth of what happened in a nutshell. Van Doorn was beating a whore in his room. She was screaming loud enough to wake the dead, and I didn't think we needed the cops taking notice of us."

"The police in Antwerp are under my control."

"Well, nobody told me that. That's something I figured out as I went. But I didn't know it then. The night I disappeared in Lisbon, I met a woman. Same thing in Tangier." Bolan turned in his seat and cast a hard stare at Van Doorn. "Why don't you ask him about that? I had to pull him away from a prostitute's door with a bloody knife in his hand, after he'd killed the doorman." The Executioner paused. It was time to take a chance. "Look, Mr. Webster," he continued, "I'm not stupid. I don't know what you've got planned, but I've picked up enough to know there's some kind of major op about to go down. I need the money. And you can use another good man."

Webster paused, finally said, "Yes, that's correct." He shrugged. "But I can't afford to take chances. Not now." He nodded toward the red-haired Irishman who'd taken a seat across the room. "That's why I recruited Mr. Duggan. A good commander always has a contingency plan, Mr. Giddings."

Ulrikson returned with a stack of bills clenched in his beefy hand. He handed the money to Bolan, the crazy, wild-eyed smile still frozen on his face.

Webster rose from his seat. "I'm sorry, Mr. Giddings. I wish it would have worked out. Hugo, please escort him to the door."

Bolan gave it one last shot. "Mr. Webster, you're making a mistake."

"I'm sorry. Hugo?"

Ulrikson reached out, taking the Executioner's arm.

Bolan stared at his hand, then up into the big Swede's eyes. "Remember what happened the last time you tried that?"

Ulrikson dropped his hand. For once the painted-on smile vanished and was replaced with an angry scowl.

The Executioner followed the man through the door, wondering where he'd go from here.

GUS WEBSTER WAITED for Ulrikson to return to the den and take a seat on the couch. "Gentlemen," he said, "the moment of truth draws nigh." He stared across the room at the big Swede. "Still nothing on Mr. Giddings's fingerprints, Hugo?"

Ukrikson shook his head. "Inspector Brabant in Hasselt is still out of town," he said. "I could try someone else...." He let his voice trail off.

Webster shook his head. "No, no. It's merely academic at this point. The problem seems to have taken care of itself." The Advance-Tech CEO indicated the door with his head. He rose from his chair and walked to the bar. "Brandy?" he said to no one in particular.

Ulrikson shook his head. Duggan held up his glass of whiskey.

"Maybe a tad," Van Doorn said, staring at the bottle.

Webster poured a thin finger of the golden liquid into a glass, walked across the room and handed it to the South African. "Deetlev," he said, "you worry me."

Van Doorn looked up, the glass halfway to his lips.

"Are you telling me the truth about your drinking?"

Van Doorn nodded. "Certainly, Mr. Webster," he said. "Hey, would I lie? To *you?*"

"I hope not. I owe you something for what you did in Angola, Deetlev. My life. For that reason, I have been lenient with you—a leniency I would not have extended to anyone else. But I do not owe you my business. A drunk and his money are soon parted, old friend. And sometimes, a drunk and his employer's money meet the same fate."

"Don't worry, Mr. Webster." Van Doorn set his glass on the table, untouched.

The Advance-Tech CEO turned to Duggan. "Your men are ready?"

"Already in place. They went in over the last three days in two's and three's. They're at the house now, waiting on the weapons."

"Excellent," Webster said. "Hugo? The rest of the supplies?"

"The weapons are across town from the men in one of your warehouses. The ammo, explosives and the rest are still here, but there should be no problem getting it to them in the country. We've bought the border."

Webster nodded. "And the uniforms?"

Ulrikson's gaze fell to the floor. He clasped his hands between his knees and lowered his head. "A delay."

Webster felt his eyes narrow. "Go ahead."

"That entire country is in turmoil at the moment."

Webster's eyebrows rose. "Tell me again where they have been assembled."

"Germany. It was the best central focus point from the various countries. But transport is unreliable. Perhaps the men could wear—"

"Hugo," Webster said, "that is impossible. It is imperative that we have *those* uniforms. Some of our men are destined to die. Their bodies will be inspected. They have to appear to represent interests other than our own."

Ulrikson nodded. "I'll check again as soon as we break."

"No," Webster said. "If transport is unreliable, then we must go get them. Prepare to fly there yourself and pick them up. Take the DC-10."

The Advance-Tech CEO looked back to Van Doorn. The South African was staring at the untouched glass of brandy on the table. "For God's sake, Deetlev," Webster said, "drink your drink."

Van Doorn took a sip, hesitated, then downed the rest.

"Deetlev," Webster continued, "I plan for you, Sean and Hugo to each lead one of the three assault teams. You were a fine soldier once. You're still up to it, aren't you?"

"Certainly, sir."

"Very good." Webster rose to his feet. "Then, gentlemen, you are dismissed. Hugo, I'll expect those uniforms here no later than the day after tomorrow."

Ulrikson and Duggan stood and filed out of the den, Van Doorn at their heels.

Webster followed them to the door. He watched the South African as he walked down the hall, wondering if the slight stagger he saw was real or imagined. "Hugo," he called down the hall.

All three men stopped in their tracks.

"Hugo, stay for a moment, please."

Duggan and Van Doorn continued past the office area and out of sight into the living room. Ulrikson returned to his side.

"Hugo, call Captain Iturbo in Belmopan. He can run Giddings's prints as well as Inspector Brabant. Tell him we must have the results as quickly as possible."

"Gus, I—"

Webster shook his head. "Another backup plan, my friend. Just in case we find Van Doorn drunk when the moment of truth arrives."

Ulrikson nodded, turned on his heel and walked into the office area.

The CEO watched him dial the number, then went back into the den. He walked to the bar, poured a half glass of the brandy and held it to his lips. His eyes fell on Van Doorn's empty glass on the table across the room. The man had saved his life, but that was long ago. Was he still capable of carrying out his duties?

Webster set the glass on the bar. He'd repaid the South African many times over for what he'd done. He was no longer indebted to the man; it was Van Doorn who owed him.

And Van Doorn would pay, if necessary.

With his life.

THE MASSIVE HEAD of the jaguar bounced in time to the potholes as Belmopan appeared down the road. Ahead, Bolan could see the colorful costumes of people dancing under the streetlights, celebrating a local festival. A combination of modern and ancient music drifted on the cool evening breeze into the open windows of the Suburban.

As they neared the city limits, red lights suddenly flashed behind them. The Executioner turned in his seat to see a Belize police car following ten yards behind.

Coba turned to him smiling, then pulled to the side of the road.

A fat officer with a five-o'clock shadow exited his vehicle and waddled toward the driver's window. "Show me your permit to hunt jaguar," he demanded in Spanish.

"My permit is Mr. Webster," Coba said as the man reached the window.

The police officer reached the window, recognized the driver and stopped in his tracks. "I am sorry, Coba," he said. "Please give the *patrón* my apologies for the delay. I didn't recognize the vehicle." The man did an about-face and returned to his car.

Bolan watched him slide behind the wheel. Just another reminder of the Advance-Tech CEO's power.

Coba pulled back onto the road and stopped at the edge of the village square. "You must get out here," the Indian driver said.

Bolan grabbed his bag from the back seat and stepped out onto the street. He walked toward the center of town, passing stands selling snakeskin products and live iguanas. Small groups of musicians stood spaced throughout the confusion, doing their best to override the sounds that floated through the air from competitive combos.

A parade of children banging worn-out tambourines and tin cans came marching down the street. Bolan stepped to the side as a ragged boy of ten passed, banging away with a spoon on a rusty car hood held by two of his friends.

The Executioner stopped a man wearing a clown's costume. *"¿Donde está teléfono público?"* he asked.

The clown took time to drink from a goatskin wine flask before speaking. "Two blocks down," he answered in Spanish. "The phone company building."

The Executioner passed more brightly costumed dancers with painted and powdered faces. Confetti flew through the air, settling on drunks who had passed out on the sidewalks. When he reached the phone company building, he spotted an ancient wooden booth set against the wall.

Bolan stepped in and closed the door behind him, drowning out most of the clamor. He dropped a coin into the slot, got the operator and, after a series of clicks and relays, soon had Aaron "The Bear" Kurtzman on the line at Stony Man Farm. "I've run into a dead end, Aaron. You picked up anything more on your screens?"

Kurtzman's gruff voice crackled as it came over the line. "Not a thing, Striker. Webster's still buying and selling, but he's hanging on to the Brownings and ammo. Also a lot of the explosives. That's big inventory and it doesn't make sense. He operates on short-term, borrowed cash, and the interest he's paying has eaten too far into his resale profit already.''

"Okay. I'll find something." He hung up.

The Executioner rose and opened the door. The city of Belmopan still looked as if it had been invaded by Roman hordes. As he stepped back out of the booth, he saw a familiar face behind the wheel of a jeep coming slowly down the street.

Van Doorn's eyes swept back and forth across the sidewalks as he crept along behind another band of marching children. The South African held the steering wheel in one hand, a gin bottle in the other.

Bolan ducked behind the booth and watched as Van Doorn hit the brakes, stopping three inches from an attractive black woman who was crossing the street. The South African leaned out of the jeep and said something, a leer on his face.

The woman looked up at him in surprise, then turned and hurried on.

Bolan stepped into the open as the jeep moved on behind the parade. The South African was up to his old tricks. He'd gotten drunk. Now he wanted a woman.

Nothing too unusual about that. Lots of men did it.

But with Deetlev Van Doorn, that drunken lust would mean a slashed throat for his victim.

The Executioner kept pace as the jeep crawled through the village. Van Doorn stopped occasionally when a woman passed in front of him, leaning drunkenly out of the vehicle to shout lewd remarks.

Bolan stayed a half block behind, threading his way through the throng of merrymakers. When they reached the center of town, Van Doorn turned left at a tall bronze statue of the Virgin Del Carmin. The jeep accelerated as the multitude of bodies began to thin.

Staying hidden in the shadows, the Executioner broke into a jog, then a sprint, as the jeep picked up speed.

Bolan had to keep up. The degenerate South African's plans for the evening were all too evident. If the Executioner lost sight of the man, there'd be a dead black woman somewhere before the sun rose.

Van Doorn was six blocks ahead when Bolan saw him turn right. The Executioner turned on the steam, feeling the sweat break out on his face and neck as his arms pumped in time to his legs. He raced to the corner, turned after the jeep and came to an abrupt halt, ducking behind a deserted tin-roofed shack as Van Doorn stepped out of the jeep.

Quickly crossing the packed-dirt parking lot, the South African opened the door of a shabby adobe cantina.

Bolan glanced at the crude, hand-lettered sign over the door. La Calevera—the Female Skull.

The Executioner crouched in the shadows, waiting. American rock and roll blasted through the open windows of the clay building. From inside, Bolan heard the crash of a bottle breaking. Three men and a woman left the bar and got into a dented, primer-painted Chevy. Their laughter faded into the night as they roared away from the parking lot and disappeared down a narrow path leading into the jungle.

A man wearing dusty tuxedo pants and a dingy white T-shirt under his suspenders came somersaulting through the door into the dirt. A moment later, a tall slender Indian with long hair walked from the bar. He kicked the man in the ribs twice, then turned and strode inside.

Fifteen minutes later, Van Doorn led a laughing Creole woman through the door. The dark, frail figure wore gold hoop earrings and faded blue jeans. Her golden skin glistened with sweat, shining provocatively against a luminous white blouse. Van Doorn and the woman stepped over the man in the tuxedo pants and walked to the jeep. The South African whispered in her ear as he opened the door, and the woman giggled again.

Bolan rose to his feet. He scanned the lot, then the rest of the area for curious eyes.

It was now or never. He couldn't keep up with the jeep on foot, and if Van Doorn got away with the defenseless woman...

Bolan sprinted across the parking lot.

Van Doorn turned as the Executioner left his feet, diving over the jeep into the back seat. The barrel of the Desert Eagle came to rest just under the South African's nose.

"What the bloody—"

"Drive," Bolan commanded.

"Giddings...shit. Look mate, can't we—"

The Executioner shoved the Desert Eagle harder against his face and Van Doorn's head jerked back. The warrior repositioned it under his chin, jamming the sight up into the soft sagging flesh. "I said *drive.*"

The woman stared over the seat, her wide eyes frozen in fear. "What are you going to—"

"Get out," Bolan barked.

He didn't have to say it twice. The woman leaped over the jeep's door with the agility of a gazelle and disappeared down the dark street.

Van Doorn shoved the key into the ignition and started the jeep. Following Bolan's orders, he backed out of the parking lot and headed toward the jungle road. "Listen, mate," he said as they reached the trees, "I can get you back in if that's what you want. I'm sorry for what I did." Tears formed at the corners of his eyes. He looked longingly at the gin bottle on the floor of the jeep.

"Turn," Bolan growled.

The South African twisted the wheel and started down the dark path leading into the jungle. "Give me a break," Van Doorn pleaded. "Please, mate. She was nothing but a kaffir."

The sobbing grew to an embarrassing wail as Bolan ordered the demented man to the side of the road. Then, as the South African set the parking brake, his sobs suddenly turned to deranged, psychopathic shrieks.

Van Doorn twisted violently in the seat, his face a mask of maniacal hatred. The Chris Reeve Jereboam knife appeared as if from nowhere, the eight-inch blade flashing under the stars toward the Executioner's throat.

Bolan pulled the trigger.

Deetlev Van Doorn jerked back against the windshield, the top of his head flying into the darkness.

Bolan pulled the body from the jeep and dragged it a hundred yards into the trees. Burying Van Doorn under a mass of dead foliage, he paused, looking up at the starry sky.

Far in the distance, he heard the music of flute and drum. In the city of Belmopan, people were happy. They danced, sang, feasted and drank wine. Later tonight they would pair off, make love, then go to sleep.

And the women of Belmopan—women the world over—could sleep a little safer with Deetlev Van Doorn in his grave.

8

La Calevera cantina looked like something out of a low-budget, post-nuclear-holocaust movie.

A naked bulb dangled from the end of an exposed wire stapled to the ceiling, its dim glow falling to the floor of packed earth. The walls were of dried mud, and an unidentifiable green fungus sprouted from within the cracks. The tables and chairs had fallen victim to the humidity years ago, rotting to wet, pliable splinters.

A dank, sour odor rose from the furniture, the cantina itself and the patrons within.

The cantina had no bar, as such. At one side of the room sat a rusty, vinyl-topped card table. Bottles and greasy gray glasses littered the tabletop. In a chair behind them sat a dark man wearing a bloodstained undershirt. He looked up grudgingly each time one of the customers stumbled over, mixing drinks and snatching the money from their hands before returning to the newspaper in his lap.

From his vantage point in the corner of the room, the Executioner tipped his rickety chair back against the wall and sipped at his room-temperature beer. A young woman wearing an embroidered peasant blouse fell into the lap of an old man at one of the tables. The man reached in his pocket, pulled out a coin and dropped it down her neckline. His hand stayed beneath the fabric, and his wrinkled eyes lighted up with the enthusiasm of a teenager.

On a shelf next to the card-table bar sat a cheap radio-cassette player. Sometime during Bolan's six-hour stay in the bar, as late night became early morning, the rock music had been replaced with the slow, eerie timbre of Peruvian flutes. Low whispers, punctuated by sudden drunken laughs, floated over the ghostly sounds.

The Executioner took another sip of his beer. La Calevera had been the perfect place for someone like Deetlev Van Doorn to spend his off hours.

Perversion was as thick in the air as the stench of the unwashed bodies.

From the corner of his eye, Bolan saw the tall Indian glaring at him again—the same tall Indian who'd beaten the man in the tuxedo pants earlier in the evening. The Indian, Mayan probably, hadn't been there when the Executioner returned to the bar after disposing of Van Doorn. He'd come back thirty minutes ago, taking a seat across the room and downing shot after shot of tequila with no visible effect.

The Executioner was closer to the man than he'd been when the beating took place. In the obscure overhead light, he saw the empty eye socket gaping in the side of the angry, sun-wrinkled face. The Indian wore his long hair loose, letting it fall over his shoulders onto a striped, coarsely woven vest.

Bolan stared straight ahead, avoiding eye contact. This man wanted trouble. He didn't. If he could avoid it, he would.

The Indian stood.

The early-morning barflies had been waiting, and their laughs stopped instantly. The whispers quieted to expectant, barely audible murmurs.

Bolan continued to stare straight ahead. No, he didn't want trouble. But if it couldn't be avoided, he'd have to do whatever became necessary.

The Executioner set the beer bottle on the table in front of him as the Indian moved smoothly across the room. Bolan's warrior eye evaluated the man in a heartbeat. Tall, lanky. Quick. Drunk, but still in control.

Mean.

All in all, little more than an overgrown bully who'd probably been right at home years ago scaring smaller children on some playground.

The Indian stopped in front of his table. "Why are you here, gringo?" he demanded.

Bolan turned toward him, finally looking into the man's eye. He shrugged and smiled. "Everyone's got to be somewhere."

The Indian's scowl deepened. He leaned forward, resting the palms of both hands on the table between them. "You're doing what you gringos like to call—" he squinted, searching for the word "—summing."

"You mean 'slumming'?" Bolan asked.

The tall man's lips curled. "Yes. Slumming. You come to watch, laugh and ridicule our poverty," he snarled.

"No," Bolan said. "I come to wait for someone."

The Indian turned his head and spit onto the table. He leaned in further, his face an inch from the Executioner's. Foul breath preceded his words. "You're a liar," he said. "You are a rich *norteamericano.* A big gringo, but like all gringos, you are a..." He squinted and waited again for the word to come. "Pussy," he finally said.

Bolan let the smile fade from his face. The time for friendliness was over. He'd given the tall Indian several chances to bow out gracefully, to retreat without losing face.

Those opportunities had gone ignored.

Without warning, the Indian reached out, grasping Bolan's lapel with both fists. Bolan let himself be hauled to his feet.

"You're staring at my eye," the Indian accused.

"What eye?"

"You mock me."

"No, friend," the Executioner said. "I'm doing my best to give you a chance to get out of here while you've still got the other one." He reached suddenly up, grasping the back of one of the Indian's wrists.

The man screamed as his wrist bent down and to the side. He made the wise decision, moving with the pressure rather than fighting against it and snapping his own joint.

Bolan followed him to the floor, kneeling on the back of his outstretched elbow as he kept the tension on the man's wrist.

The Indian's breath came in quick, painful pants. He stared at the ceiling, petrified.

"I'm going to let you up now," Bolan told him. "Don't be stupid. Go home. Or sit back down and leave me alone. Will you do that?"

The man's head bobbed up and down.

The Executioner dropped the man's arm, stood and took a step back.

The Indian sprang back to his feet like an alley cat. His lone eye glowered at the Executioner as his hand disappeared under the vest.

Bolan retreated another step as ten inches of razor-edged steel flashed a quarter of an inch from his nose.

Before the lanky man could move again, the Executioner stepped in. He blocked a backhand, follow-up slash with his left arm and sent a solid right cross driving into his opponent's nose.

The man fell to his back, blood spurting from both nostrils. The solitary eye opened wide, blinked twice, then closed.

Bolan sat back down and took a sip of his beer as the conversation around the bar resumed. The bartender and another man were dragging the Indian toward the door when a hulking form wearing a huge revolver and Viking battle-ax suddenly blocked the entrance.

The clamor in La Calevera faded once more.

Ulrikson stepped to the side, letting the men drag the Indian through the opening. The ever-present smile covered his face as he scanned the room. His eyes fell finally on the Executioner. For a moment, the grin thinned.

The big Swede strode across the room to Bolan's table. "Giddings."

Bolan looked him in the eye. "Nice of you to remember."

The big man laughed out loud. "I'm looking for Van Doorn."

Bolan nodded, took another drink of beer and said, "I know how you feel. I've done my share of it."

"Where is he?"

Bolan shrugged. "How should I know? I'm no longer his keeper."

The big Swede placed both hands on his hips above the weapons worn openly on his belt. "Why are you here?"

The Executioner let himself smile. "Funny," he said, pointing toward the door. "Another guy just asked me the same thing."

Ulrikson's gaze narrowed. "This is curious. Why don't I believe you about Van Doorn?"

"I don't know." The Executioner lifted his bottle again. "But it's your problem, not mine."

In one smooth movement, Ulrikson unsnapped the sheath at his waist and drew the battle-ax. He held the weapon in both hands to the side like a baseball bat. "You have no idea how much pleasure it would give me to chop you to pieces, Giddings. And perhaps I will before the night is through. But for the time being..." He indicated the door with his head.

Bolan rose to his feet and dropped several bills on the table. Ulrikson followed him out the door.

"Where are we going?" he asked the Swede as they got into the Suburban.

"To see Webster." Ulrikson replaced the battle-ax as he slid behind the wheel, then turned to face Bolan. "You'll talk to him," he said, patting the massive weapon within the sheath, "or you'll talk to *this*."

GUS WEBSTER OPENED his eyes to see that it was Hugo Ulrikson's hand rousing him from his sleep. The big Swede held a steaming mug of coffee in his other meaty fist.

Webster frowned in displeasure. He'd been having the most delightful dream. Sigourney Weaver, Kim Basinger and Jamie Lee Curtis had just begun to remove his clothes.

Now all he saw was a big, bulky Swede.

Webster rubbed his eyes with both hands. He considered sending the intruder away, but he was never able to recapture the same nighttime fantasies once he'd been awakened.

And besides, he reasoned as his mind continued to clear, Ulrikson wouldn't have disturbed him unless something had gone wrong. Very wrong.

Webster sat up and took the coffee. "Yes, Hugo," he said hoarsely, "what is it?"

"Van Doorn's missing."

"And what's so unusual about that, Hugo? Have you tried his usual haunts? Any kaffirs, as he calls them, turn up with their throats cut?"

"He's nowhere to be found, Gus."

Webster sipped at the coffee while Ulrikson explained about finding Giddings in the bar on the edge of Belmopan. When the big Swede had finished, the Advance-Tech CEO swung his legs over the side of the mattress and reached for the powder blue silk robe hanging on the chair next to the bed. "So, I'm given to believe that you feel Mr. Giddings is in some way responsible for Deetlev's disappearance?''

Ulrikson nodded. "I can't come up with any other explanation, Gus. Giddings didn't like being let go. We knew that. What better way to get hired again than to create his own opening?''

Webster stepped into the robe. "Quite possible," he said. "Particularly right now, when he knows something of importance is about to occur. On the other hand, Hugo, our friend Deetlev had any number of enemies who'd like to see him—''

"I don't think so, Gus.''

"You say Giddings is here now?''

"In the den.''

"Well,'' Webster said, yawning, "let's see what he has to say.''

The Advance-Tech CEO slid into his slippers and followed Ulrikson down the hall to the den. He paused at the door. Dawn was breaking through the windows. He stared past the mounted animals to the couch against the far wall where Giddings sat in the half-light. The man's face was devoid of emotion, but somehow, he looked far more dangerous than the snarling beasts that crowed the room.

Webster switched on the overhead light and shuffled to the chair across from Giddings. He drank the last of the coffee and handed Ulrikson the empty mug.

Without being told, the big Swede left the room.

Webster looked at Giddings again. "Good morning.''

"Good morning.''

Ulrikson appeared at his side and handed him a fresh, steaming mug. "So, Mr. Giddings, what do you have to say for yourself?"

"Absolutely nothing. I don't work for you anymore."

Webster felt the anger boiling up inside him. This man was different than Ulrikson, Duggan and Van Doorn. Particularly Van Doorn.

Giddings had a mind of his own.

He forced himself to remain calm. Giddings's ability to think for himself was irritating, but it was a characteristic that could prove useful in the upcoming mission.

"All right, Mr. Giddings," he said. "Fair enough. But let me explain something to you. You will not leave here alive unless you tell me what you know about Van Doorn's disappearance."

The big man on the couch didn't bat an eye. "Then I guess I'm free to go now," he said, "because I've already told your little Viking buddy here what I know. Nothing."

Webster had opened his mouth to speak when the phone on the table next to him suddenly rang, piercing through the tension in the room like a stiletto to the throat. He nodded to Ulrikson.

The big Swede lifted the receiver. "Yes?" There was a long pause. "Yes, Captain. Yes. I'll inform Mr. Webster. Thank you." Ulrikson hung up and turned to Webster.

"That was Captain Iturbo," he said. "Van Doorn was found early this morning by a woodcutter. He's had his head blown off."

Webster felt relief flood through his body. At last. Van Doorn's actions in the jungle years ago had made it difficult for him to rid himself of the drunken South African. Now, someone had done it for him.

He turned back to Giddings. "I will give you one more chance, Mr. Giddings. Did you kill Van Doorn?"

Bolan stared back at him without speaking.

"All right," Webster said. "In reality, it makes no difference. If you are responsible, it shows a bit of enterprise, and a great deal of ambition on your part. If you are not, I still need someone to replace Van Doorn. Mr. Giddings, you are rehired."

"And suppose I'm no longer interested?"

"Well," he said, "are you or aren't you?"

Bolan paused a moment. "Yes."

"Good." Webster could see Ulrikson's discomfort. That was good, too. Having Giddings around would ensure the big Swede stayed on his toes. "Then I have an assignment for you. You've already guessed that we have a large-scale op about to go down. We're having trouble getting the uniforms that will be worn. They're an eclectic bunch—fatigues from Russia, web gear from Britain. The boots are coming from Thailand. It's important that anyone who falls during the mission not be representative of any country or interest. The gear has been assembled in Germany, but we're having trouble getting it out. I had planned to send Hugo—" he glanced toward the Swede "—but I can make better use of him here. I want you to fly there immediately. See that the equipment gets back here."

"That's fine," Bolan replied. "But I haven't slept all night. How about if—"

"You'll be able to sleep on the plane." Webster rose to his feet. "The DC will be busy, and the other planes are too small for the freight. You'll have to fly commercial. Rent a cargo plane once you take possession of the merchandise in Germany and return it here." The Advance-Tech CEO ran a hand through his hair. "Hugo, take Mr. Giddings to Duggan. Tell your Irish friend to brief him. Need-to-know only. Then return here at once."

A few minutes later, the big Swede reentered the room. He opened his mouth to speak.

Webster held up his hand, stopping the words before they came out. "Relax, Hugo. We need a man like Giddings, but I'm not hiring him blindly. Did Iturbo have the results of his fingerprints when he called?"

"No. He's wired Washington, but they haven't gotten back to him. We should have an answer soon, though."

"Excellent."

Ulrikson paused, then said, "I'm a little confused, Gus. *I* was taking the DC-10 to Germany. So what's this about it being busy all of a sudden? Where's it going?"

Webster chuckled. "To Germany. And you're going with it as planned." He sipped once more at his coffee. "Another contingency plan, old friend. We're going to find out once and for all if Al Giddings is the man he claims to be."

COBA'S LONG GRAY PONYTAIL flapped in the wind from the Suburban's open window. Sweat formed in tiny beads on his forehead. The Indian had left the air conditioner off, obviously preferring the heat to which he was accustomed.

Bolan studied the hard lines of the old man's face as they neared the airport. Coba didn't look stupid. He had to be aware of what was going on. He and the other Indian workers were involved in the same illegal activity as Webster.

But the Indians were victims as well as perpetrators. Like the coca farmers who supplied the cocaine cartels of South America, they'd grown up in poverty. They'd been forced to choose between crime and starvation. In essence, between survival and death. Not justification for their actions, maybe, but at least an explanation.

Webster, Ulrikson, Van Doorn and Duggan had no excuse but greed.

The Suburban slowed as they turned onto the drive leading to the terminal. Bolan saw the plane waiting on the runway in the distance. He was all too aware that nothing would be gained by going to Germany. What he had to do was infiltrate the office at Webster's compound. Somewhere within those glass walls lay the secret about the mission Advance-Tech was about to launch.

Tourists carrying luggage and souvenirs, dressed in walking shorts and T-shirts bearing the names of Central American resorts and hotels, crowded the front of the terminal. Bolan pulled his carryon over the seat and stepped out into the heat. He walked swiftly toward the front entrance, watching the Suburban drive away in the reflection from the window.

The Executioner threaded his way through the crowd inside, scanning the room. Webster had made reservations for him to Belize City, then on to Caracas, with a connecting flight to Berlin. He turned to the window and saw the Suburban roll onto the drive leading to the highway. At least Coba wasn't watching him. But it was highly probably that someone from Advance-Tech was. He still hadn't advanced past his informal probationary period, and Webster wouldn't be taking chances. Someone would make sure he got on the flight.

Bolan's gaze fell on a row of telephones against the far wall. He moved quickly through the crowd, fishing in his pocket for a coin.

Someone would be watching. That meant that Al Giddings's seat would have to be filled. All the way to Berlin. And once there, someone would have to pick up the uniforms.

Someone would, but it wouldn't be the Executioner.

Bolan leaned against the cool clay of the wall as he gave the operator Hal Brognola's office number. Two minutes later, he had the Justice man on the phone. "I'm still fishing," he said. "Anything new on your end?"

"Negative, Striker."

"Okay," Bolan told him. "Here's the predicament." Briefly he ran down the situation with the uniforms, aware that he was taking chances on an unsecure line. "I can't afford to waste time in Germany, Hal. I need somebody to fill in for me."

"Let's get Kurtzman on it," Brognola said.

A series of clicks snapped across the lines, then the Executioner heard Bear's familiar voice. "Kurtzman."

"It's Hal. I've got Striker on the line. Aaron, check those magic disks of yours and find us someone who looks reasonably like him. We need a stand-in."

"Hang on," Kurtzman said. "I'll tap into personnel."

The light tapping of computer keys at the other end of the line was the only sound for several minutes. Then, "Got a lulu for you. Alcohol Tobacco and Firearms man. Two inches shorter, but it's as close as we get. Former Marine LRRP. Same hair color, and he can lose his mustache."

"What's his name?" Bolan asked.

"Vann," Kurtzman answered. "Sid Vann."

"Good enough," Bolan said. "Get him shaved." He paused. "Bear, what's Grimaldi's status?"

"We've had him on hold in case you needed him."

"Great. Have him fly Vann to Caracas. Tell them both to meet me in front of the Aeroperu counter. Vann can take my seat to Berlin, and I'll thumb a ride back here with Jack."

"So where do *you* go from there?" Brognola asked.

The Executioner thought briefly of the animals in Webster's trophy room. "Back into the lion's den."

THE STARS SPARKLED like diamonds as the Executioner fell through the sky. Above him, Jack Grimaldi and the Stony Man aircraft disappeared into the clouds.

Bolan hit the ground running, jerking hard on the parachute lines, and drew the silk inward. He let his mind drift back over the lightning-paced events of the past few hours as he folded the chute into a tight square.

After stashing his weapons in a locker at the Belize City airport, he'd filled his seat to Venezuela. Grimaldi and Sid Vann had been waiting when his flight had touched down. While the tall, muscular BATF agent would never pass a close-quarters inspection in his role as Al Giddings, the resemblance had been enough to startle even the Executioner. Chances were good that Webster's connection in Germany had only a general description of him, which meant that with a little luck, Vann's cover wouldn't get blown.

And if luck wasn't with them...

It was a calculated risk that had to be taken.

From Caracas, it had been the whirlwind flight back to Belize to retrieve the Beretta and Desert Eagle, then the short flight to Webster's compound.

Bolan finished folding the chute and anchored it under a large rock. His trained eyes scanned the clearing under the bright full moon. The wind had shifted suddenly as he dropped through the night, altering his fall. He'd maneuvered the lines with the skill of experience, finally come to earth in a clearing a half mile farther west of the ranch house than he'd planned.

The Executioner flipped the cover on his watch and stared down at the luminous green hands. Nearly midnight. If he was lucky, Webster and the rest of the men occupying the bedrooms in the house would be asleep.

The warrior jogged across the clearing. The massive Desert Eagle .44 Magnum slapped quietly against his hip as he ran. The Beretta 93-R, sound suppressor screwed firmly into the end of the barrel, rode snugly in shoulder leather under his arm. On the other side of the X-rig harness, its razor-edged blade hidden by a black plastic sheath, hung a Cold Steel Magnum Tanto fighting knife.

Bolan wore a skintight black combat suit. Hidden in its many pockets were extra magazines for both weapons and a small black flashlight. Black combat cosmetics covered the skin of his face, hands and neck.

Entering the jungle, Bolan used the knife as a machete, chopping his way through the thick foliage. It was 23:45 by the time the lights of the guard shack appeared through the trees.

The Executioner dropped to all fours, slowly paralleling the road to the gate. The soldier's survival senses went on alert as he neared the first obstacle.

Two men stood leaning against the gate, smoking cigarettes. Bolan slowed his pace even more, creeping silently through the leaves and vines until he drew abreast. The razor-wire fence extended from the gate out of sight into the trees. The Executioner pulled a multipurpose tool from a pouch and used the sharpened teeth of the wire cutters to snip his way through. He reached out gingerly with one hand, blindly searching the darkened ground. His fingertips brushed the cool steel wire of the trip line three feet from the fence, ankle-high.

With a quick glance back at the guards, Bolan stepped over the line and moved on through the trees.

It was midnight by the time he reached the ranch house. Bolan circled the grounds, staying just inside the tree line until he stood across from the back patio to the den. He watched a jeep carrying two men with M-16s drive slowly past, the heavy beam of their searchlight sweeping back and forth across the gravel road. As soon as they disappeared around a curve, he dived face-first to the ground and crawled to the patio.

The alarm system mounted next to the sliding glass door posed no problem for the Executioner. He pulled the flashlight from his combat suit and covered the bulb with his hand, working swiftly by the eerie orange-red light that glowed through his flesh. As soon as the device had been neutralized, he slipped the blade of his knife between the door and the frame.

The sliding door screeched maddeningly as Bolan inched it open. He froze, once more listening for the slightest change in his environment. Satisfied that he hadn't been heard, he slid through the opening and closed the door behind him.

The lions, tigers and other animals snarled in death as the Executioner crept past them to the hall. He stopped at the door, pressing his back against the wall.

Somewhere at the other end of the house, he heard the slow, steady snores of someone sleeping.

Bolan clutched his knife firmly in an ice-pick grip, the shiny steel blade hidden from view behind his forearm. His rubber-soled combat boots moved silently down the hall to a bathroom. With a quick look inside, he crept across the carpet to an open door.

The Executioner peered around the corner and saw the source of the snores. Gus Webster lay peacefully in his bed, sleeping the slumber of the innocent.

Bolan moved on to the next bedroom. Peering through the opening, he saw twin beds. Duggan lay on his side in the one closest to the door. The bedspread on the other was still tucked neatly over the mattress.

Ulrikson. Where was he?

The Executioner retraced his steps down the hall to the office. Sheathing the Tanto, he reached for the doorknob, then froze.

Behind him, he heard the springs creak. Then heavy footsteps padded toward him.

Bolan moved across the hall and froze once more, his back to the wall. A moment later he heard the lid to the toilet clank against the tank, then a steady stream as either Webster or Duggan urinated into the bowl. A few seconds later, a hoarse, phlegmy cough echoed down the hall, then the toilet flushed and the footsteps retreated once more.

The Executioner crossed back to the office door. A tiny flash of silver caught his eye through the glass wall. Cupping the flashlight in his hand, he peered through the glass to see a thin metal wire running up the side of the door.

Another alarm.

Bolan stepped back and took a deep breath. It had to be activated somewhere on this side of the door. But where? He ran the flashlight along the door frame. Nothing. The alarm could be anywhere in the house, and searching for it would eat up valuable time better spent in the office. He was about to begin the time-consuming task when bedsprings sang from the hall again. This time the footsteps were steady, purposeful, as they headed toward him.

The Executioner ducked back into the den. A split second later, he saw Webster move past the door and lift a painting from the wall. The Advance-Tech CEO's hand disappeared into a hole the picture had covered. A buzzer sounded softly, and a moment later the door to the office swung open.

Bolan watched as Webster took a seat behind his desk, picked up the phone and tapped at the numbers. He yawned as he waited for the line to connect.

A few seconds later, he said, "Iturbo? Webster. Yes," he said sarcastically, "I'm well aware of the time. But not hearing from you is interrupting my sleep, so I might as well interrupt yours." There was a long pause, then he said, "Iturbo, I don't give a rat's ass about anything but results. Get me what I asked for, or you'll wind up offshore with about fifty pounds of iron chain taking you down to the Caribbean floor. You got it?" He hung up.

Bolan watched as Webster returned to the hall, closed the door and reactivated the alarm before replacing the painting. The Advance-Tech CEO disappeared back down the hall.

The Executioner waited several minutes, then crept to the picture. Lifting it from its hook, he set it on the floor and pulled the flashlight from his pocket.

The alarm was a simple device—an on-off toggle switch. Bolan flipped it, and the office door opened once more.

The Executioner went to work quickly, hitting the computer's power switch, then searching through the folders in the metal file cabinets as the machine programmed itself. Finding nothing of interest, he turned back to the machine as it clicked, indicating its readiness. He tapped the "list files" button for the hard disk, and a moment later several dozen coded titles appeared on the screen.

Bolan's fingers flew over the keys as he began the tedious task of searching the menu. His mind raced as he checked each entry. Guns to the Red Brigades; explosives to other terrorist groups in central Europe, Africa and Japan; a mobile RLW "robot tank" to a clandestine group secretly sponsored by the Iraqis.

Webster's dealing with the savages of the world went on and on as the Executioner scanned the screen, creating his own mental files for future reference as he went.

A half hour into the search, Bolan called up a document simply entitled "Fernandez." A cold chill suddenly coursed through his veins as the Executioner began reading the first of a series of letters.

The Executioner hit the Page Down key and dropped to the letter's signature—Jaime Fernandez, leader of the Farabunde Marti National Liberation Front, a cover organization for different antigovernment groups in El Salvador. Better known to the world as "The Butcher."

Bolan returned to the body of the letter in which Fernandez proposed a joint operation between Farabunde Marti and Advance-Tech, with no less at stake than the country of Costa Rica. Fearful of U.S. reprisal if his group worked aboveground, the Butcher suggested that Webster recruit men from around the world. FMNLF would take care of the politics, planting false clues of discontent in Costa Rica that would eventually culminate in a violent overthrow by the "people of Costa Rica" themselves.

Bolan skimmed through the remaining paragraphs, then moved to Webster's reply. The Advance-Tech CEO agreed—with one stipulation. When the smoke cleared, he intended to be sitting behind the desk in the president's palace.

Webster had told Bolan at their first meeting that he had bigger aspirations. But not even the Executioner had guessed how big.

Gus Webster intended to become a king.

The rest of the letters worked out the details. Originally set for earlier in the year, the mission had been postponed. Bolan searched through the letters again.

Nowhere was there a clue as to the new timetable.

The Executioner sat back and stared at the screen. There *had* been recent rumors of unrest in Costa Rica. Fernandez had done his job.

Perhaps the only stable political environment in Central America, Costa Rica was a haven for many Americans, particularly elderly couples seeking a peaceful, agreeable climate in which to spend their remaining years. The economy being what it was, many retired people lived well on small pensions that would have been eaten up in the States.

Old people. Defenseless. How many would die when the fighting broke out in the streets?

And besides the Americans, how many Costa Ricans would fall under the fire of "their people"?

Bolan switched off the computer and stood.

None. Not if the Executioner had anything to say about it.

9

Gus Webster drew a lungful of Havana smoke into his chest and let it trail slowly from his nose and mouth. He watched the thin wisps rise lazily to the living room ceiling, then turned his eyes back to the window.

Far down the gravel road, the Suburban rounded a curve and proceeded toward the house. As the vehicle neared, Coba's coarse, wrinkled face took shape behind the wheel.

Next to him sat the man who'd been calling himself Al Giddings.

The fire in his chest had begun earlier in the day, when Ulrikson had briefed him. Now it intensified, as outrage flooded his soul. He fought against the sudden urge to rise from his seat, draw the .38 from his hip and put a bullet in the impostor's brain as he mounted the front steps.

Captain Iturbo still hadn't gotten back to him. He'd have had the bastard's head on a silver platter by now, except that it no longer mattered what name was attached to Giddings's fingerprints.

Whoever Al Giddings was, he *wasn't* Al Giddings. He was some kind of cop or government agent.

Webster saw movement to his side and turned to see Ulrikson enter the living room.

The Swede glanced through the glass as the Suburban pulled to a halt in front of the house. He shook his head. "Gus, you know I don't like to argue with you. But this is a mistake. Why not just kill the bastard the second he steps through the door?" He patted the battle-ax in the sheath on his belt.

Webster shook his head. "No, Hugo. We've got to assess the damage first. Whoever the American stand-in was, he was an agent of some kind, too. There's no telling how much they know and have told their confederates. We can't just kill Giddings outright. Not anymore." The Advance-Tech CEO paused to draw once more on the cigar. "Al Giddings has got to disappear."

"Then at least let *me* handle it, Gus. Duggan's good, but I'm—"

"Indispensable," Webster finished.

"That wasn't what I was going to say—"

"No, perhaps not. But it's true. I need you here, Hugo. If Giddings somehow happens to escape the trap, I can afford to lose Duggan. Not you." Webster watched the smile return to the big Swede's face.

A moment later, the door opened. Coba ushered Bolan inside. "Ah, Mr. Giddings," Webster said. The impulse to kill the man returned. He wanted to reach out, clasp the man around the throat and strangle him with his bare hands.

Webster forced a smile and studied the big man head to foot. No, even if it was practical politically, facing Giddings man to man wouldn't be such a good idea.

"You've done an excellent job."

Bolan shrugged. "There wasn't a lot to it."

Webster nodded. "Perhaps not in your estimation, but you've proved your reliability. So much so that I've got another job..." He let his voice trail off. "Enough for now—I'm getting ahead of myself. I understand the uniforms and other equipment are on their way here now?"

"The Indians were loading the trucks when we left the airport."

"Fine." Webster turned to the big Swede. "Hugo, find Sean, and then the two of you join us in the den." Motioning Bolan to follow, he turned on his heel and walked down the hall.

In the den, Webster took his usual chair and waved Bolan toward the couch. He draped an arm around the neck of a stuffed cougar at his side and puffed again on the cigar.

Ulrikson and Duggan entered the room and took seats on one of the other couches.

The Advance-Tech CEO nodded to both men and began. "I'll get straight to the point, gentlemen. An emergency of sorts has arisen. A simple matter to correct, actually, but annoying nonetheless. And it couldn't have come at a more inopportune time." He stared across the room at Bolan as he continued to puff on the cigar. "Mr. Giddings, are you familiar with the name José Guttman?"

"I've heard it before."

Webster nodded. He'd picked the name out of the morning paper. It added an air of authenticity to what he was about to say. "A left-wing Managuan newspaperman. He's created small problems for me in the past."

Bolan remained silent.

"Well," Webster continued, "he's finally gone too far. I have reason to believe he has information about our upcoming operation." The Advance-Tech CEO cleared his throat. "Information that would prove disastrous if it turned up in print."

The phone on the table next to him rang. Webster started to pick it up, then looked toward Ulrikson. The big Swede crossed the room, lifted the receiver and placed it against his ear.

"I want you to accompany Sean to Nicaragua and eliminate the threat, Mr. Giddings. You'd better get started." Webster rose to his feet.

To his side he heard Ulrikson say, "Yes, Captain. Certainly. Thank you."

Webster escorted Bolan to the hall. "When you return, Mr. Giddings," he said, "I'll brief you myself concerning the mission. You'll be playing a major role, and you'll be paid well for it."

Bolan looked him in the eye. "You've kept me in the dark every step of the way so far," he said. "Be honest with me for once. I'm tired as hell. Am I going to get a chance to sleep before this big deal—whatever it is—goes down?"

Webster forced a laugh. Without thinking, he glanced at his watch. "Only if you hurry," he said. "We're planning—" The Advance-Tech CEO suddenly caught himself.

There was more to Giddings's question than met the eye. The bastard was trying to get a fix on his timetable.

Webster cleared his throat. "I'll brief you when you return." He turned away from the penetrating eyes. It was a million-to-one shot that Giddings would live through the night, but there was still no point in taking chances. "Sean," he said, "take Baxter and Haneline with you. You won't need the DC, and Baxter can fly the Cessna. Make sure the job gets done right."

Bolan followed Duggan out of the room.

As soon as they were gone, Webster turned to Ulrikson. Nodding toward the phone, he said, "Captain Iturbo?"

The big Swede's head bobbed nervously up and down. He seemed to be having trouble swallowing.

"Well?" Webster said.

Ulrikson shook his head. "You won't believe it. Giddings's real name is . . . Mack Bolan."

The red-hot anger in Webster's veins suddenly turned to ice water. "The Executioner," he heard himself breathe. The Advance-Tech CEO felt his hands begin to shake. He walked to the bar and poured three fingers of cognac into a snifter.

Mack Bolan. The Executioner. The ex-Special Forces veteran who had spent his life single-handedly defying everyone from the Mafia to the KGB, from terrorists to drug cartels.

Webster downed the cognac in one swift gulp. He turned back to Ulrikson. "Okay," he said. "Go on to Costa Rica. Get the men organized and ready." As the fiery French brandy made its way from his stomach to his brain, the fear of the man known as the Executioner began to fade. Bolan was only a man. One man.

One man who'd be dead before the night was through.

Webster looked up at Ulrikson. "Get everything ready. Duggan and the others will take care of Bolan."

"Gus, what if—"

He held up a hand. "Relax, Hugo. By tomorrow morning, the bastard will be rotting away in Managua." He paused, and the thrill of upcoming victory, wealth and power filled his soul—inhibited only slightly by the uncertainty that remained in his chest. "And you and I, Hugo, will own a country."

SINCE THE FIRST STONES of the city had gone up in the last century, Managua, Nicaragua, had been awaiting disaster.

Because their city was built atop layer upon layer of volcanic mudflows, ash, cinders and pumice, the people of Managua kept one eye permanently open, pointed fifteen miles to the south—toward the Volcan Masaya. Centuries earlier, the giant volcano had been worshiped as a god.

The people of modern Managua revered it only slightly less.

The Managuans ate, slept and worked over one of the largest faults of the Cocos Plate, and so the threat of earthquakes was never far from their minds. The rumblings beneath their feet took a close second on their list of fears.

In the twentieth century, a new form of terror was added to the people's nightmares: civil war.

Bolan watched the sun fade over the Pacific as the Advance-Tech Cessna made its final descent toward Managua. From the ground below, a gaseous mist swirled up toward the plane. Bolan looked down and saw the eight craters forming the volcano gape back at him like the mouths of giant, fire-breathing dragons.

A few moments later, the wheels hit the runway. Bolan heard a wheezing gasp for air behind him. He glanced over his shoulder at the man sitting next to Duggan. With the exception of Haneline's asthmatic puffs, and the fact that Baxter was piloting the aircraft, the two men could have been two peas in a pod. Both were in their early forties, had dark hair, battle-weary faces and were engaged in a losing contest with the middle-age overhang that had begun to creep over their belts. They'd said hello to the Executioner upon meeting him, then remained quiet during the flight.

Bolan turned back to the windshield as the Cessna rolled to a halt. A blue Land Rover raced in their direction across the runway, followed closely by a black-and-white police car. As the Executioner dropped to the tarmac, both vehicles stopped, and uniformed men stepped out.

Duggan moved forward to the Land Rover and shook hands with a fat man wearing lieutenant bars. Sweat glistened on his corpulent cheeks and fell in steady drops from the tails of his long Zapata mustache. He smiled hugely as he accepted an envelope from Duggan, then handed the Irishman a set of keys before returning to the cruiser.

The police car sped back across the runway as Baxter and Haneline transferred the weapons from the plane to the Land Rover. The two men got in the back, Duggan slid behind the wheel and Bolan took the shotgun seat.

The vehicle pulled away from the airport. Soon they were cruising through the outskirts of Managua, passing new apartment and office buildings. As both the financial center of the country and Nicaragua's youngest city, Managua seemed never to grow old, being periodically destroyed by either warfare or natural disaster, and then rebuilt.

A small, lighted baseball diamond caught the Executioner's eye. The bleachers were packed with spectators, but instead of cheering on men in caps and cleats, their eyes were glued to two fighting cocks spurring each other to death in a ring drawn around home plate.

On the other side of the street, the Nicaraguan version of the bullfight was under way. The matador had leaped onto the bull's back and now rode the fierce animal around the ring in triumph.

The festive mood changed as they neared the central district of the city. Moonlike vacant lots, their ashy soil gleaming like quartz in the starlight, now spotted the scenery. Unlike the suburbs, little attempt had been made to rebuild. Rubble and debris was the theme of Managua's central core.

Leaving the city, Duggan pulled the Land Rover up an access road onto the highway leading toward Lake Managua. Bolan watched him from the corner of his eye. The Irishman wasn't as verbose as Van Doorn had been, but he wasn't a mute, either. He'd been uncharacteristically quiet since their departure from Belmopan, and neither Baxter nor Haneline had spoken. It had given the Executioner time to think.

And work on solutions to the two major problems now facing him.

First, he had to find a way to prevent the assassination of José Guttman. The newspaperman might be a screaming crybaby idealist with no foothold on reality, but that didn't mean he deserved to be murdered.

Second, it was imperative that he contact Brognola again. By now, Sid Vann would have passed on the information that the operation Webster had mounted was nothing less than the overthrow of Costa Rica. Brognola would already be putting together the military strike force Bolan had called for.

But the man from Justice would also have followed the Executioner's recommendation that the U.S. forces go on alert, rather than enter Costa Rica immediately. Bolan had still had no idea when Webster's invasion was set to take place when he'd met with Vann.

The Land Rover continued on through the night, passing cotton fields and cornfields until the strong odor of the fresh-water lake filled their nostrils. Duggan turned off the highway onto a dirt road running along the lake.

Bolan knew that American troops would never be allowed to stay in Costa Rica for long. With the political climate what it was in Central America, Costa Rican officials couldn't afford to alienate their neighbors by permitting it. And liberal American congressmen would start working on withdrawal the moment they learned of American intervention. That meant that if the strike force went in too early, all Webster and Fernandez would have to do was postpone their onslaught until the troops were withdrawn.

Bolan watched Duggan from the corner of his eye as the man punched the lighter in the dash, then held it to the cigarette protruding from his mouth. Things had changed quickly. Webster had let down his guard, if only for a second. He'd inferred that the mission would begin soon. Very soon. Which meant that the invasion might be over, and the mock government in place, before the U.S. even learned about it.

It was time to get word back to the U.S. Start moving in the troops. But how? When? Duggan hadn't let him out of his sight since the last meeting.

Which brought a third potential problem. Something smelled incredibly wrong to the Executioner as they continued to drive along the lake. The scattered houses popping up along the shore were elaborate. Far too expensive for the average American, even in the Costa Rican economy. And they'd cost more than a socialist South American journalist like Guttman would make in a lifetime.

Bolan settled back against the seat as one of his problems disappeared. Wherever they were headed, it wasn't to kill José Guttman.

But with the solution to that dilemma, another emerged. Webster hadn't sent them to Nicaragua for the good weather. And they'd come prepared for battle. In addition to their personal weapons, Webster had issued each man one of the full-auto Browning Hi-Powers and 200-round drum mags.

They had come to kill someone. And it was obvious to Bolan who the most likely victim would be.

Duggan pulled to the side of the road and killed the lights. "From here on in, we're on foot," he announced. He turned in his seat, resting an arm over the back. "Haneline, issue the ordnance." The Irishman waited until each man held a stock-extended Hi-Power in his lap, then continued. "Here's the plan. We go down the road to the house. Giddings, you and I'll take the front. Baxter, you and Haneline cover the back. When you hear us kick the door, we all go in and we waste the bastard. Now, is that simple enough?''

Bolan nodded. Baxter and Haneline both grunted.

Slowly they made their way down the narrow road. When the lights of the house appeared in the distance, Duggan stopped. He held up a hand, pointed to Baxter and Haneline, then waved them toward the rear of the house.

Bolan stayed at his side as they moved toward the front door. Lights shone brightly behind the closed curtains. Unless the Executioner missed his guess, this house, like so many others, belonged to Webster.

It might be unoccupied, but he couldn't discount the possibility that more men would be inside.

In any case, Duggan, Baxter and Haneline wouldn't make their move until they were through the door. If they'd planned to kill him on the road, they'd have already tried. Inside, he'd be trapped.

At least that's what they were counting on.

Bolan took his place next to the door. He kept one eye on Duggan. The first few seconds would be crucial. What he had in mind would require split-second timing. He couldn't kill Duggan—he had to keep him alive for information about the Costa Rican invasion.

And he had to stay alive himself. If he could.

When Duggan nodded toward the door, the Executioner lifted a boot and kicked.

Bolan went through first, diving forward onto his belly the moment he crossed the threshold. As he'd expected, a burst of automatic fire sailed over him as he hit the floor. The bullets flew on across the room, shattering the glass from a framed picture hanging over the fireplace.

The Executioner heard the back door crash open as he rolled to face Duggan. A gasp of surprise blew from the Irishman as his momentum carried him forward to trip over Bolan. The Executioner reached up, grabbed Duggan's jacket and pulled.

The Irishman's Browning went skipping across the carpet. A short jab with the stock of Bolan's Hi-Power drove Duggan's head into the carpet. Another sharp strike shattered the Irishman's teeth and closed his eyes.

The Executioner was back on his feet in a heartbeat. Two halls, one on each side of the fireplace, led away from the front room toward the rear of the house.

He chose the one to his right. The Browning leading the way, he moved to the door and pressed his back against the wall. Peering around the corner, he saw Baxter creeping toward him, his autopistol gripped in assault carry mode. Haneline stood behind him, facing away to cover their rear.

The Executioner stepped around the corner, leveled his weapon and tapped the trigger. A 3-round burst of 9 mm slugs blew Baxter's scalp from the top of his head.

Haneline ducked out of sight through the door.

Bolan crouched low, making his way slowly down the hall. When he reached the door, he dropped to one knee and stuck the tip of the Browning's barrel into the opening.

A sudden volley of rounds blasted through the night, glancing off the warrior's pistol and sending it flying from the Executioner's hands.

Bolan drew back and jerked the Desert Eagle from his hip.

Haneline's familiar, wheezing breath drifted eerily into the hall. Then Bolan heard footsteps patter away from him across the floor. Rising to his feet, he risked a look.

The kitchen. Empty.

Cautiously the Executioner stepped into the room, the big .44 Magnum gripped firmly in both hands. A door leading to the back, the wood around the lock splintered and broken, stood open on one hinge. Another door on the opposite wall opened to the hall on the other side of the house.

The Executioner moved slowly across the kitchen. As he reached the hall, a soft tap drew his gaze upward.

A trapdoor led to the attic. Bolan reached for a dangling cord and jerked. The trap opened and a rickety set of stairs unfolded to the floor. At the top of the steps, a bushy-haired head peered into the opening, as well as the probing muzzle of a 9 mm autopistol.

Bolan fired twice, and the body of a hardman tumbled down the steps. The Executioner had started up the stairs when he heard a faint, muffled wheeze from the kitchen behind him.

Haneline. The Advance-Tech gunner had circled the house through the living room and come up on his rear.

Bolan dived from the steps to the floor as a steady stream of 9 mm parabellums sailed over his head. Rolling to his side, he brought up the Desert Eagle.

Haneline stood in the middle of the kitchen, firing through the doorway with his right hand. The Advance-Tech gunner's left was clamped over his mouth in a futile attempt to stifle the telltale gasps.

Bolan leveled the Desert Eagle and fired. A 240-grain, jacketed hollowpoint sped from the .44's barrel at 1,180 feet per second, slowing only slightly as it drilled through Haneline's hand, then into his brain.

Suddenly the house fell silent.

The Executioner moved quickly up the stairs to the attic. He fired three rounds through the opening as he reached the top, then stuck his head up, swiveling a fast 360-degree scan. Empty.

Back in the kitchen, he found a water glass in the cabinet, filled it at the sink and returned to the living room. He dumped the water over Duggan's face and waited.

A moment later, the Irishman's eyes opened, his lips sputtered and he rose painfully to a sitting position, his hands clasped to his swollen face.

Bolan dropped to one knee and shoved the Desert Eagle into the hollow just above the Irishman's collarbone. "We need to talk."

Duggan moved his hands from his face, and a red and purple eye stared up at the Executioner. "I think I'm gonna puke."

Bolan thrust the gun in harder against his throat. "Fine. Just don't do it until you've told me what I want to know."

Duggan nodded. "Hell, whatever you say. I got no love for Webster. It's just a job to me."

"Let's start with how they figured out my name's not Giddings."

Duggan smiled, his broken, bloody teeth making him look like an evil jack-o'-lantern. "Ulrikson followed you to Germany. Saw the guy you duked in. That answer your question, Mr. Bolan?"

Bolan frowned. "And how'd they learn that?"

"Got your fingerprints off a glass or plate or something."

The warrior studied the Irish terrorist. Every step of the way on this mission, he'd been reminded of the corrupt power Gus Webster wielded. At every airport and dock, the officials had been paid off. The police in Belgium, Morocco, Belize, and now Nicaragua, all seemed to ask "How high?" each time the Advance-Tech CEO ordered them to jump.

And now it appeared he even had links into the confidential files of the Justice Department. A check on "Al Giddings's" fingerprints *should* have verified Bolan's cover. Security had somehow been breached. Brognola would have to do some housecleaning.

The Executioner turned his attention back to Duggan. "When's the op in Costa Rica set to come off?"

"It's already starting."

"What?"

"That's right. The men have been in place for days. Ulrikson's on his way there now to start the show. I'm supposed to meet them there just as soon as..." The Irishman's voice trailed off as he realized what he'd almost admitted. "Listen," he said, his tone suddenly less confident, "I was only taking orders. Hell, you been a soldier. You know how that goes. What do you say we bury the hatchet and take off on our own? You're good, man. And I've worked with everyone from Khaddafi to the IRA. With my connections, we could rustle up enough business to both get rich.''

"Let me think about it." Bolan rose to his feet and shoved the Desert Eagle back in the holster. "I've got a call to make."

The Executioner glanced quickly at the .45 auto still in the holster of Duggan's hip. Turning his back, he walked toward the phone on the coffee table across the room.

Behind him, he heard the quiet rustle of clothing. "Hell, there's no limit to what we could do together," the Irishman said. Bolan heard the faint crack of leather as the man quietly unsnapped the retaining strap on his holster.

Picking up the phone receiver, Bolan tapped the area code, and first four numbers for Brognola's office. To his rear, Duggan coughed, and above the cough the warrior heard the sound of cold steel sliding against leather.

"They really call you the Executioner?"

The Beretta 93-R flew from under Bolan's arm to his hand as he whirled. A 3-round burst of suppressed 9 mm slugs flew from the weapon to drill through the Irishman's swollen face.

"Yeah, they do."

10

Bolan kept the Cessna low over the mountain slopes surrounding San José. Below, patches of forest and coffee plantations dotted the hillsides, casting macabre shadows across the craggy terrain under the moon.

The Cessna's wheels hit the tarmac, and the Executioner saw the unmarked sedan waiting under the lights at the end of the runway. The plane slowed as it neared the vehicle.

Two men stood flanking the sedan. One was short, stocky and swarthy, wearing the khaki uniform of the Costa Rican police.

The second face was familiar, and the Executioner couldn't help but smile as he dropped from the door of the Cessna to the ground. For a brief moment, he had to wonder if U.S. Navy SEAL Lieutenant Jesse Oven had even changed clothes since their last meeting a few months ago.

The mat-black Sig-Saur automatic and a row of extra 9 mm magazines still dangled from a web belt around Oven's waist. A well-worn desert camouflage uniform covered his sinewy body, and crisscrossed over the blouse were two ammunition belts carrying extra rounds for the Stoner M-63 A1 machine gun gripped in his hands. A floppy jungle hat sat atop his head, completing the outfit Bolan remembered from their mission to Cuba, in which the Executioner had held off Fidel Castro with a portable "backpack" nuke provided by the SEAL.

Oven stood in salute as Bolan crossed the tarmac to the vehicle.

"Let's forget about formalities, Lieutenant," Bolan said. "We've got an invasion to stop."

"Fair enough." Oven grinned. "By the way, it's Captain now." The scrappy Navy SEAL opened the door and Bolan slid into the back seat. "I'll brief you on the way, Belasko," he said, using the cover name the Executioner had operated under during the Cuban affair. He took the seat next to Bolan as the dark-skinned San José cop jumped behind the wheel.

Bolan glanced down between them. A Heckler & Koch MP-5 with a 30-round magazine rested on the seat. Next to it was a web vest with extra mags shoved into the pockets. Six fragmentation grenades hung from metal hooks on the front.

"Merry Christmas," Oven said, then tapped the driver on the shoulder. "Let's go, Sergeant."

The driver threw the sedan into gear and they took off across the runway to the street.

"Let's have it," Bolan said, slipping into the vest.

Oven settled back in his seat. "Two, maybe three hundred men. Moving toward the government buildings in the national park from three sides."

"Ours?" Bolan asked.

Oven laughed. "I only wish. We were lucky to get a hundred troops. Mostly my men, but a few Green Beanies came along. They're okay—for guys who can't swim."

"What was the hangup?"

"The usual—politics. The Man in the Oval Office had a hell of a time getting us off before news reached certain senators the way it was." He paused and drew in a deep breath. "We only have a hundred men, Belasko. As you might guess, the bulk of our men are in the Mideast. But what we've got, they're the best."

"You in charge?"

"Was until you got here. That comes straight from the White House, too." The smile on the man's face changed to a curious frown. "Someday, when we get time, you want to tell me who the hell you really are?"

Bolan chuckled. "Considering the conditions we always meet under, Oven, we'll never have time. You set up defenses yet?"

"In progress." He pulled a map from his shirt pocket and spread it across his lap. "Turn on the overhead, Sergeant." The light switched on, and Oven jabbed at the paper with a thick forefinger. "You want the good news first, or the bad?"

"Give me the bad."

"Like I said, we're outnumbered. At least three to one. But the good news is that they're marching right down the center of the damn streets. At first I thought they were crazy. Then it began to make sense. According to what you told Brognola, they're trying to make this look like a group of Costa Rican revolutionaries, organized by the people themselves. So they're counting on getting there before help arrives. Anyway, I've got three teams of twenty-five each, hidden at points along the mercs' route. The National Theater, the museum, and an indoor aviary building called the Union Club." Oven stopped, pulled his hat off and mopped sweat from his forehead with the back of his cuff. "We're heading toward the theater now."

"What else?"

Oven tapped a spot on the map a quarter inch from the National Theater. "Another group of mercs has already made it to the presidential palace. Moved in before we could set up. Some of them have been trying to cross the street—presumably to blow the gates. Local forces are having a hell of a time, but so far, they've held them off." Oven refolded the map and stuffed it back in his pocket. "We're getting set to launch a rear assault and catch them in the cross fire."

"That all?"

Oven nodded. "It's enough for me." He looked up at Bolan and shook his head. "It's your dog-and-pony show now, Belasko. What do *you* want to do?"

Bolan remained silent. The driver turned onto Paseo Colon and raced down the wide street, passing curious onlookers. Costa Ricans gathered near the curbs, whispering and pointing toward the center of town.

"Looks like they've just passed," Oven said.

The Executioner pointed toward the walkie-talkie on the SEAL's hip. "Get your man at the theater on the air," he ordered.

Oven ripped the walkie-talkie from his side and held it to his lips. "Kingfish to Piranha, Kingfish to Piranha. Talk to me, Jackie."

A moment later, a hushed voice came back over the crackling airwaves. "Piranha. Go."

"Give me your location."

"Just past the National Theater," the man whispered. "Got company coming to visit, fast. Hundred yards and moving steady."

Bolan motioned for the radio.

"I've got somebody who wants to talk to you." Oven paused and looked quizzically at Bolan.

"Striker will do," Bolan said.

"Call him Striker," Oven said into the mike. "He's in charge. Follow his orders as if they were mine."

Bolan took the instrument and tapped the button. "How many men you facing, Piranha?"

Static danced over the air, then cleared as the man on the other end keyed the mike and said, "Seventy, Striker, maybe eighty, tops."

Oven turned and watched Bolan as the Executioner answered. "We're bringing up the rear. Wait till you hear our fire. Then open up."

There was a pause at the other end of the airwaves, then the voice said, "Begging Striker's pardon, sir, but is it just the two of you at the rear?" Another pause, then, "This sailor would advise you not to try to—"

Oven grabbed the walkie-talkie and keyed the mike, cutting him off. "Thanks for the wet-nursing, Piranha. But don't worry about us." He snorted through his nose and grinned up at the Executioner. "I've got a whole army with me you don't even know about."

As they reached a long line of office buildings, the driver suddenly slowed. Through the windshield, Bolan saw several dozen of Webster's mercs dressed in the eclectic fatigues Vann had obtained in Germany. In their hands were more of the full-auto Browning Hi-Powers with wooden shoulder stocks. Marching informally in an unstructured company, they moved boldly down the middle of the street, singing loudly in Spanish and bearing huge signs announcing, *"¡Liberación!"* and *"¡Emancipación!"*

Several of the men at the rear of the mob turned around as the sedan drew up behind them. They laughed, raised their fists, shouted *"¡Libertad absoluto!"* and turned back to the front.

Bolan watched. It was obvious they were expecting no resistance.

Oven shook his head in revulsion. "El Bullshit," he spit.

Bolan tapped the driver on the shoulder. "Here's where we get out."

The driver pulled to the curb. His voice shook as he spoke. "Costa Rica is *my* country," he said in Spanish. "I will go with you."

Bolan looked him up and down. Fat hung in huge folds over his black Sam Browne belt. A blue-worn Taurus .38 and a cartridge carrier bearing twelve extra rounds hung from his hip—the man's only armament. More importantly, sweat seemed to gush from every pore of his frightened face, contradicting the offer he'd just made and betraying his true desires.

The Executioner shook his head. "You have a radio in this thing?"

The sergeant nodded and pointed toward the glove compartment.

"I need you back at the airport," Bolan said. "More of the enemy may land anytime. We'll need to be advised."

Relief flooded through the fat man's eyes. He nodded.

Bolan drew back the bolt of the MP-5 and slammed a cartridge into the chamber. Turning toward Oven, he said, "You ready?"

Oven nodded. "I may be a captain now," he said, "but I'm a workin' boss." He shoved the 15-round drum magazine into the Stoner. "Let's rock and roll."

Bolan rolled out of the vehicle onto the ground, the H&K already hopping in his hands as he hit the ground. Three men at the rear of the column fell face-forward to the street.

The sergeant behind the wheel of the sedan threw the vehicle in reverse and backed away from the skirmish. The Executioner heard a steady string of fire from the M-63, and in his peripheral vision saw Oven firing from a prone position near the curb.

A block in the distance, front fire from the American troops at the National Theater sounded through the night.

Bolan squeezed the trigger again, and another row of Webster's revolutionaries-for-hire fell to the cold concrete of Paseo Colon. As he traded the empty box mag for a fresh load, the rest of the marching men turned, confusion and fear highlighting their features under the streetlights.

A hardman with red hair and a full, bushy beard raised his autopistol and fired, the speeding 9 mm rounds chipping the concrete next to where the Executioner lay.

Bolan rolled to his side and tapped the trigger once more, a 3-round burst of parabellum cutting into the man's chest. He shot backward as if propelled from a cannon, knocking two more Advance-Tech mercenaries to the ground.

Both Bolan and Oven bore down on the triggers of their weapons, sending steady streams of ammo drilling into the mob. The men still standing bolted for cover, their angry signs proclaiming phony freedom falling to the pavement.

From ahead in the street, more rounds drilled through the night as the American soldiers at the theater downed the enemy from the front.

Three mercs foolishly sprinted forward toward Bolan and Oven. The Executioner caught the first with a single round through the right eye. Oven took the second, sending a blast of fire from the Stoner stitching up and down the man's fatigues.

The third member of the trio froze in his tracks. The Executioner and the SEAL downed him with rounds from both weapons.

As the streets cleared, a lone man stood a hundred yards away, calmly raising the SA-7 missile launcher in his hands.

Bolan leveled the H&K and squeezed.

A short burst blew into the merc's chest. His arms flew upward as he pulled the trigger, and the missile burst skyward, illuminating the sky like a fireworks display.

The surviving mercs had reached the cover of the office buildings on the other side of the street. Sporadic fire now assaulted Bolan and Oven from doorways, alley corners and one rooftop.

The Executioner rolled to his feet, sprinting a zigzag around the corner of the closest building. He dropped the partially spent magazine from the H&K and rammed a full load into the well. A split second later, Oven dived down next to him. Blood spurted from the SEAL's thigh like the stream of an opened fire hydrant.

Oven looked up and waved a hand in front of his face. "I'm okay."

Bolan knelt next to him, ripping the fatigue trousers away from the wound. A clean hit. Through and through.

From the other side of the building came sporadic fire. The Executioner hurried to the corner and glanced around the bricks.

The American troops had advanced and were moving in and out of the doorways in mini search-and-destroy missions. Two jeeps followed slowly, the .50-caliber machine guns mounted just behind the seats sweeping back and forth across the street on their turrets.

Bolan saw a group of Advance-Tech mercs crowded into a doorway directly across the street. Yanking a frag grenade from his vest, he pulled the pin and heaved the bomb into the opening.

The Executioner didn't wait to see the results. He heard them, both the explosion and screams, as he returned to Oven. Tearing several long strips from the SEAL's fatigue blouse, he hurriedly field-dressed the wound, tightening the knots before helping the man back to his feet. Oven started to fall and the Executioner caught him.

"Let's get you some help," Bolan said.

"Dammit, Belasko," Oven growled. "I said I was okay."

The Executioner dropped to one knee and peered around the corner of the office building again. The firing from behind the other buildings quieted as a combined force of twenty SEALS and Green Berets crept cautiously down the center of the street.

Oven leaned against the wall and held the walkie-talkie to his face. "Kingfish here," he growled into the mike. "Hold your fire. Striker and I are coming out."

Bolan and Oven stepped from behind the building. Twenty M-16 A1 assault rifles turned in their direction, then redirected toward the sky.

The Executioner half carried Oven toward a SEAL wearing a camouflage bandanna around his forehead. "Get him to the medics, sailor," he ordered.

"Like hell," Oven said. "Listen, you pulled this shit on me in Cuba. If you think I'm going to just fade away into the sun—"

Bolan shook his head. "With all due respect, Captain . . ."

The Executioner's right cross fell solidly on Oven's jaw. He caught the man as he slumped toward the pavement, passed him on to the SEAL in the bandanna and raced to the nearest jeep.

A young sergeant with kinky blond hair under his Green Beret looked up as the Executioner slid into the passenger's seat. "Striker?"

Bolan nodded. "And you?"

"Waken, sir."

"All right, Waken, what's the situation at the rest of the sites?"

"We're kicking ass at the National Museum and the Union Club," Waken reported. "The locals are still holding them off at the president's palace, but we're having a time of it getting our men into position." He tapped the radio between them on the seat. "Evidently they've got most of their men concentrated there, led by some big asshole who looks like Thor."

Bolan felt a hard smile touch his lips. "Then let's get to the palace. Get on the horn and tell the rest of the troops to clean up their messes and meet us there."

The young Special Forces soldier grinned. He threw the jeep into gear and tore off down a side street as the remaining Americans continued to probe Paseo Colon for remnants of Webster's troops.

HUGO ULRIKSON WATCHED the ongoing battle outside the president's palace. Things hadn't gone exactly as he'd planned.

The Swede ducked into a doorway as a volley of automatic rifle fire ricocheted off the wall next to him, forming a cloud of dust from the clay building. Looking overhead, he read the sign, which in Spanish said Department of Motor Vehicles.

He pressed his back against the door and took a deep breath. So far they hadn't even been able to cross the street to blow the palace gates. Somehow, the Costa Rican government had gotten advance notice of the invasion, and American troops had arrived almost as soon as his own men had attacked.

Ulrikson stared down at the watch on his arm as more rounds exploded outside. Duggan should have been here by now, which meant he wasn't coming at all. He was dead.

And his death, in turn, answered the question of how the Americans and Costa Ricans had learned of the invasion.

Mack Bolan. The bastard they called the Executioner.

A shiver shot up Ulrikson's spine. He'd heard tales of the Executioner, and some said the man was indestructible.

The big Swede clamped his teeth and felt his jaw tighten. Bolan was only a man. He could be killed.

And before this night was over, Hugo Ulrikson would be the man who did it.

Steady fire drove him farther back against the wall. Ulrikson smiled, in genuine mirth rather than habit. The Americans were obviously outnumbered. It was just a matter of time. Perhaps their presence could even be put to good use. When the dust settled, he and Webster could denounce their actions, then forgive them and form a new alliance with the United States. It wouldn't be the first time the U.S. had conveniently switched sides after a coup proved to be successful.

Ulrikson leaned out of the doorway, squeezed the trigger of his Browning and sent a burst of fire into the windows on the second floor of the president's palace. Somewhere, behind those walls, the present leader of Costa Rica huddled in fear, awaiting death.

The big Swede laughed out loud. He'd never met El presidente. He had nothing against the man.

But death was exactly what he'd give him.

Suddenly an explosion sounded, and the night lighted up outside the doorway. Ulrikson peeked out and saw the building next to him burst into flame.

A convoy of new jeeps, police cars and armored troop carriers roared down the street toward the palace. An American Green Beret stood in the back seat of the lead jeep, reloading a bazooka.

Ulrikson ducked back as the Special Forces man sent another round exploding into the building. The concussion traveled through the wall, jarring the assault pistol from the big Swede's hands.

The shiver raced down Ulrikson's back once more. The odds had suddenly changed. What had looked to be a battle that could be won with time was now about to become a slaughterhouse. His slaughterhouse.

A quick mental image of Gus Webster, safe and secure in his den back in Belize, flashed through the big Swede's mind. Webster hadn't seen fit to jeopardize his own ass on this operation. Why the hell should Ulrikson risk his?

Hugo Ulrikson made a quick decision. There was no way he could serve as vice-president of Costa Rica from a coffin.

Drawing the Super Mag from his holster, he sprinted from the building a split second before a third round from the bazooka obliterated the doorway where he'd stood.

A U.S. Navy SEAL leaped from one of the oncoming jeeps and raised his M-16. Ulrikson drilled a booming .357 Maximum through the sailor's chest. He snapped three more rounds in the direction of the oncoming convoy, then cut down the narrow alley between the buildings. Halfway to the corner, he saw a dark figure dart from the side of the building, twisted and fired twice.

The percussion from the massive weapon echoed off the walls of the alley as the slugs ripped through the gut of a man in camouflage fatigues.

A wood-stocked Browning fell to the ground.

Ulrikson raced past the fallen man, barely noticing that he was one of his own.

Reaching the end of the alley, the big Swede bolted onto a side street just as a jeep squealed around the corner. He caught a quick glimpse of the Green Beret behind the wheel as the vehicle's front fender glanced off his thigh and sent him spinning to the curb on the other side of the street.

Ulrikson heard the screech of rubber as the driver stomped on the brake and skidded to a halt ten feet past him. He hit the ground in a judo fall and rolled expertly back to his feet, the Super Mag gripped in both fists.

Next to the Green Beret, he saw Mack Bolan turn to face him.

Ulrikson dropped the sights of the Super Mag on Bolan's head. He saw the man lunge for the Heckler & Koch MP-5 in his lap and laughed.

Bolan would never make it in time.

Many men had tried over the years, but it was Hugo Ulrikson who was about to become the man who killed Mack Bolan, the Executioner.

The hammer fell on the Dan Wesson Super Mag a split second before Bolan could bring around the MP-5.

BOLAN GRIPPED THE RADIO MIKE as they sped toward the palace. Oven's voice crackled over the airwaves. "I'm patched up and on my way to join you, Striker. And don't argue."

"You sure the leg's up to it?"

A snort came over the radio. "My jaw hurts worse than the leg, you bastard."

Bolan laughed. "What's the report from the museum and the Union Club?" he asked.

"Same as the theater," Oven came back. "We kicked ass and now we're rounding up the stragglers. Captured two more SA-7s and a whole shitload of explosives. And the tide's turned at the palace. Everyone scattered when the heavy guns showed up. We're taking a lot of prisoners, Striker. These cowards hadn't planned on facing any real resistance. Most of them are begging to testify against Webster in exchange for immunity."

"Good enough," the Executioner said as Waken guided the jeep around a corner. "I'll meet you at—"

Suddenly a bulky figure darted out of the alley behind a government building. Waken's foot flew to the brake, and the MP-5 in the Executioner's lap sailed up against the dash, then fell to the floor between his legs.

Bolan flew forward, rebounding against the front of the jeep before jerking back in the seat as the vehicle screeched to a halt. He felt the slight bump as Hugo Ulrikson spun off the fender and out of sight behind him.

Bolan twisted in the seat as he bent toward the MP-5 on the floor. His hand found the subgun's pistol grip as the gaping eye in the end of Ulrikson's Super Mag settled, staring dully back at him.

Too late.

Ulrikson's fingers tightened around the revolver. The cylinder began to rotate.

In the microsecond it took him to swing around the H&K, choppy mental images raced past the Executioner's eyes. The death of his mother, father and sister at the hands of the Mafia. His war—first with that same Mafia, then the KGB, drug dealers and terrorists.

Bolan felt no remorse. He'd fought a good fight.

As he continued to bring the MP-5 into play, Bolan saw the Dan Wesson cylinder complete its turn. And with a dull, metallic click, the hammer fell on an empty brass casing.

The Executioner leveled his subgun on Ulrikson's chest and stepped down from the jeep.

The plastic smile finally vanished from Hugo Ulrikson's face. In its place, Bolan saw the vicious, demonic glare that seemed to light the big Swede's eyes with fiery coals. Ulrikson pulled the trigger twice more, then drew back his arm and sent the huge piece of steel rocketing through the air toward Bolan's head.

The Executioner stepped calmly to the side, letting the Super Mag fly by to crash into the door of the jeep.

Ulrikson pointed to the MP-5. "You're a coward," he yelled. "You won't face me, man to man."

Behind him, Bolan heard the bolt slide home on Waken's M-16. He raised a hand, stopping the man. Turning, he tossed the H&K up to the Green Beret.

"Sir, I don't think—"

Bolan turned back to Ulrikson.

The fire in the big Swede's eyes intensified as he unsnapped the sheath, drew the Viking battle-ax and raised it to shoulder-level with his right hand.

Bolan jerked the Cold Steel Magnum Tanto knife from his belt as Ulrikson started to circle.

"You'll die the way the enemies of my ancestors died," the big Swede spit.

Ulrikson continued to threaten the warrior as he circled. Then suddenly, in midsentence, he lunged, raising the battle-ax higher before chopping viciously down at the Executioner's head.

Bolan shuffled a half step to the side, letting the curved blade sparkle past under the streetlight.

Ulrikson's own momentum carried him forward, off balance.

The Executioner moved in as the big Swede stumbled, catching him on the wrist with the Tanto's armor-piercing point.

Ulrikson bellowed like a bull with a sword in his hump. Blood shot from the severed artery in his arm. He twisted back, bringing the ax around in an arc toward Bolan's throat.

The Executioner backpedaled as the blade whisked past his neck. Ulrikson charged, driving him farther to the rear and trapping him against the door of the jeep. The big Swede raised the battle-ax once more, preparing to drive it down into the Executioner's skull.

Bolan reached up, catching the man's wrist just below the grip of the weapon and driving the Tanto straight forward like a punch to the chest.

Ulrikson blocked the knife and wrapped his fingers around the Executioner's wrist.

Sweat poured from the faces of both men as the battle of strength began. Bolan pushed with all his might against Ulrikson's arm, struggling to keep the ax from plummeting down to crush his skull.

Ulrikson held tight to the Executioner's wrist, pushing back, the Tanto's razor point an inch from his chest.

The muscles in Bolan's shoulders and back screamed in agony as he fought against the advantageous angle of the taller man. But slowly, millimeter by millimeter, the ax began to descend.

Bolan twisted the Tanto in his fingers and pressed the blade against Ulrikson's arm, sawing back and forth.

More blood dripped from the shallow incisions, doing no real damage except to draw the big Swede's attention.

The warrior took advantage of the distraction.

Suddenly releasing the tension against Ulrikson's arm, the Executioner twisted to the side. The bearded blade of the battle-ax swept down, slicing through his shirt at the shoulder before penetrating deep into the door of the jeep.

Ulrikson bent forward with the movement. Gasping in surprise, he jerked on the grip of the wedged ax. The weapon didn't budge.

Bolan held on to the Swede's arm and, using it for leverage, he drove his head down into the man's jaw.

Ulrikson howled in pain, but held on.

Again and again The Executioner jerked down, catching his adversary on the jaw, the chin, the ear, as the enraged Swede struggled to free the ax. Bolan felt the cartilage in the man's nose crumble under his forehead, and blood showered from his nostrils to splatter both men.

Ulrikson's breaths came in short, shallow pants. In desperation, he released Bolan's knife arm and lunged for the battle-ax with both hands.

The Executioner stepped forward, bringing his blade up, deep into Ulrikson's sternum.

The big Swede staggered back. Bolan followed, twisting the blade, and Ulrikson fell to the ground, his wild eyes staring vacantly skyward.

Bolan leaned back against the jeep to catch his breath as another jeep pulled to a halt beside him.

Jesse Oven stepped painfully from the vehicle and limped forward, his leg wrapped in gauze and adhesive tape.

The Navy SEAL captain took a quick look at Ulrikson, then turned to face the Executioner. "Can't you ever let me in on *anything,* Belasko?"

THE MIDDAY SUN shone down through a cloudless sky, seeping through the cracks in the dense branches and leaves. The black combat suit covering Bolan's body soaked up the Belize jungle heat like a dry sponge. The Executioner barely noticed. His mind was focusing on his task.

Retracing the same path he'd taken the night he broke into Webster's office and first learned about the Advance-Tech CEO's diabolical plan, Bolan paralleled the road until the razor-wire fence showed through the trees.

Ten feet from the guard shack, Bolan stepped from the foliage onto the road. As the guards scrambled to meet this threat, the warrior fired off three precise shots that took out the opposition.

The Executioner continued down the road to the house. A few minutes later, he heard the sounds of a vehicle approaching from the rear. Ducking back into the trees, he peered through the branches as the Suburban rounded a curve and passed.

Bolan stepped back onto the road and raised the Beretta. Another barely audible 9 mm round pierced the back window of the vehicle before racing into the brain of the driver. He pulled the corpse from the vehicle, slid behind the wheel and drove on.

The ranch house appeared in the distance. Bolan parked the Suburban, mounted the front steps and rapped on the door with the heavy barrel of the Desert Eagle.

The door swung open. Cabo stared at him in horror, the brown, wrinkled skin of the old Indian's face turning gray.

Bolan hooked a thumb over his shoulder. "Get out of here."

The grateful man's face softened with relief. He hurried past the Executioner and down the steps.

Bolan closed the door behind him and walked through the living room to the hall. As he passed the glass wall of the office, he heard Webster's voice from the den.

"Who is it, Cabo?"

Bolan held the Desert Eagle in front of him as he stepped into the room. "Retribution."

Webster's head shot up in surprise. The Advance-Tech CEO sat in his usual chair among the trophies. A thick cigar was pressed between the middle and index finger of one hand, and in the other he held a brandy snifter. A .38 automatic rested in a suede, inside-the-pants holster on the table next to him.

The same anxious expression Cabo had shown flashed briefly on his face, then disappeared. "Ah, Mr. Bolan. Come in."

"I'd planned to." Bolan took a seat on the couch, keeping the Desert Eagle leveled on Webster's chest.

"Mr. Bolan, I did not get where I am by being foolish. I was prepared in case the mission went sour." He paused to draw on the cigar. "I always have a contingency plan."

Bolan sat back against the couch, fighting the desire to yawn. He knew what was coming. He'd heard it hundreds of times during his lifelong war.

"Please look inside the briefcase on the bar."

The Executioner rose and walked to the bar. He searched quickly around the case for wires, then flipped the catches and opened the lid.

Carefully wrapped stacks of hundred-dollar bills met his eyes.

"It's yours, Mr. Bolan. And it's only the beginning. You have always impressed me with your abilities. And now, with my top men gone, I need you more than ever."

Bolan turned to face him. "How much is inside?"

"Five hundred thousand dollars. And like I said, it's only the beginning."

The Executioner nodded. "Thanks. I'll take it."

Webster's smile broadened. A quiet sigh of relief blew through his lips, and the rest of the tension disappeared from his face. "A wise move. I knew what I had heard about you was wrong. I knew you had to be intelligent. And no wise man passes up money." The Advance-Tech CEO took a sip of his drink, then set it on the table next to the .38. "Now, the first order of business is to make sure the men captured in Costa Rica do not testify against me. You will go directly to—"

Bolan cut him off. "Sorry, but I don't have time to listen to this."

Webster's face reddened in anger. "What do you mean?"

"I've got an important appointment. Got to be on my way."

Webster stood, placing his hands on his hips. "Perhaps you didn't understand. We are not *partners*. You work for me. No appointment is so important that you just walk out on me. Just who is it with?"

"Friend of yours," Bolan said. "Jaime Fernandez. The one they call the Butcher."

The color faded from Webster's face as realization set in. "Then they were right," he whispered. "You can't be bought. At any price?"

"No."

Webster lunged for the .38, but he never got it out of the holster.

Bolan squeezed the trigger, and the big .44 Magnum pumped two rounds through the Advance-Tech CEO's chest.

The Executioner knelt over Gus Webster as the man's body jerked with its final few breaths. "No," he said. "I can't be bought." He rose to his feet, walked back to the bar and refastened the briefcase. Holding it at the end of his arm, he paused a final time over Webster.

"But thanks for the money, anyway."

Gus Webster didn't hear. His body had quit contorting and lay still on the floor.

Bolan left the house and returned to the Suburban. Tossing the briefcase into the back seat, he fired the big engine to life and started back down the road.

Only four Americans had given their lives in San José. As casualties went, that was light.

It was still four too many.

Money could never take the place of those four brave soldiers, but five hundred thousand, split four ways, would alleviate some of the financial strain the deaths brought on their families.

Bolan turned onto the highway and pressed down on the accelerator. He glanced at his watch. Grimaldi should be circling the Belmopan airport, getting ready to land. Stony Man's ace pilot would then fly him to El Salvador, where he could begin his search for Jaime Fernandez.

Webster had been wrong. It *was* an important appointment.

And Mack Bolan had no intention of missing it.

Bolan goes head to head with a renegade dictator.

DON PENDLETON's
MACK BOLAN®

What civilization has feared most since Hitler is about to happen: deadly technology reaching the hands of a madman. All he needs to complete his doomsday weapon is a missing scrambler component. But there is a major obstacle in his way—The Executioner.

Mack Bolan's mission: intercept the missing component and put an end to a bloody game of tag with fanatical cutthroats.

Take
4 explosive books
plus a
mystery bonus
FREE

Mail to: Gold Eagle Reader Service
3010 Walden Ave.,
P.O. Box 1394
Buffalo, NY 14240-1394

YEAH! Rush me 4 FREE Gold Eagle novels and my FREE mystery gift. Then send me
4 brand-new novels every other month as they come off the presses. Bill me at the low
price of just $13.80* for each shipment—a saving of over 10% off the cover prices! There
is NO extra charge for postage and handling! There is no minimum number of books I
must buy. I can always cancel at any time simply by returning a shipment at your cost or by
returning any shipping statement marked "cancel." Even if I never buy another book from
Gold Eagle, the 4 free books and surprise gift are mine to keep forever.   164 BPM AEQ6

_____
Name   (PLEASE PRINT)

_____
Address   Apt. No.

_____
City   State   Zip

_____
Signature (if under 18, parent or guardian must sign)

*Terms and prices subject to change without notice. Sales tax applicable in NY. This offer
is limited to one order per household and not valid to present subscribers. Offer not
available in Canada.

Justice Marshall Cade and his partner, Janek, continue to bring home the law in Book 2 of the exciting new future-law-enforcement miniseries...

MIKE LINAKER

It takes a new breed of cop to deliver justice in tomorrow's America—a ravaged world gone mad.

In Book 2: HARDCASE, a series of seemingly random murders puts Cade and Janek on to a far-reaching conspiracy orchestrated by a ruthless money manipulator and military renegades with visions of taking over the U.S. government and military.

Available in September at your favorite retail outlet.
